ABOUT THE AUT

Born in New York in
grew up during the De
15½ to go to work, and
had made his first fort
bankrupt for over a million dollars and had to
begin all over again. When he was 30, and
having risen to the position of executive director
of budget and planning for Universal Pictures,
Harold Robbins began to write. NEVER LOVE
A STRANGER (1947) became an immediate
bestseller. Five novels later, in 1960, Robbins
faced a decision: his writing or a business career.
For him there could be only one choice. He has
since become one of the world's best-selling
writers, many of his novels have been filmed,
and his books have been translated into almost
every language.

Harold Robbins now has homes in the USA,
Mexico and the South of France, dividing his
time between writing, and research for his
novels.

*By Harold Robbins
and published by New English Library:*

NEVER LOVE A STRANGER
THE DREAM MERCHANTS
A STONE FOR DANNY FISHER
NEVER LEAVE ME
79 PARK AVENUE
STILETTO
THE CARPETBAGGERS
WHERE LOVE HAS GONE
THE ADVENTURERS
THE INHERITORS
THE BETSY
THE PIRATE
THE LONELY LADY
DREAMS DIE FIRST
MEMORIES OF ANOTHER DAY
GOODBYE, JANETTE
SPELLBINDER
DESCENT FROM XANADU
THE STORYTELLER

NEVER LEAVE ME

Harold Robbins

NEW ENGLISH LIBRARY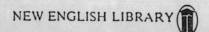

First published in Great Britain by
Robert Hale Limited in 1956
Copyright © 1956 by Harold Robbins

First NEL edition June 1968
Reprinted November 1969
Reprinted August 1971
New edition January 1972
New edition January 1973
Reprinted March 1974
New edition June 1975
Reprinted November 1975
Reprinted January 1977
New edition October 1977
Reprinted August 1978
Reprinted June 1979
Reprinted July 1980
Reprinted April 1981
Reprinted January 1982
Reprinted April 1984
Reprinted February 1985
Reprinted July 1986

NEL Books are published by
New English Library,
Mill Road, Dunton Green,
Sevenoaks, Kent.
Editorial office: 47 Bedford Square, London WC1B 3DP.

Printed and bound in Great Britain by
Hunt Barnard Printing Ltd., Aylesbury, Bucks.

0 450 00067 8

THE END AS THE BEGINNING

It was two-thirty when I got back to the office after lunch. My secretary looked up as I came through the door. 'Those contracts get here from the lawyer yet?' I asked.

She nodded. 'I put them on your desk, Brad.'

I went on into my office, sat down behind my desk and picked them up. I riffled the sheets of paper with my fingers. These tightly typed pages with all their crazy wherefores and whereases was the real McCoy. The big time. I couldn't help but feel the glow of satisfaction through me as I began to read them. It was better than brandy after dinner.

The buzzer hawked and I picked up the phone, still looking at the contract. 'Paul Remey, calling from Washington, on two,' my secretary's voice whispered in my ear.

'Right,' I said, pressing down the button. The satisfaction had eased into my voice. 'Paul,' I said into the mouthpiece, 'I got the contract in my hand –'

'Brad!' His voice was harsh, interrupting, and there was something in it that set my heart suddenly pounding with fear.

'Yes, Paul?'

His words burned into my brain. 'Elaine committed suicide!'

'No, Paul!' The contract slipped from my fingers, spreading its white sheets over the desk and floor. There was a tight band around my chest. Twice I tried to speak and twice I failed.

I slumped back into my chair. The room was beginning to spin vaguely around me. I closed my eyes. Elaine, I cried silently – Elaine, Elaine, Elaine.

Desperately I forced myself to speak. My voice was cracked and strange to my ears. 'How, Paul? When?'

'Last night,' he said. 'Sleeping pills.'

I took a deep breath. My self-control was coming back. 'Why, Paul?' I forced myself to ask, but I knew the answer. 'Did she leave a note?'

'No note. Nothing. Nobody knows why.'

A small sigh of relief escaped my lips. The kid had played it straight right down to the wire. My voice was stronger now. 'It's a terrible shock, Paul.'

'To all of us, Brad,' he said. 'Just when everything seemed to be working out for her, too. Just a few weeks ago Edith was saying how happy Elaine seemed, now

6

that you were helping on that Infantile drive. She said Elaine had found herself again, doing something for others.'

'I know,' I said wearily. 'I know.'

'That's why I called, Brad,' he said. 'Elaine was so fond of you. She thought you were the greatest. She was always telling Edith how wonderful you were to her.'

There was pain coming from his words. I had to stop him from talking like that, or he'd kill me. 'I thought she was pretty wonderful too,' I said huskily.

'We all did, Brad,' he assured me. 'We all wondered where she got so much courage from, the strength to face all the things she had to. Now I guess we'll never know.'

I closed my eyes. They'll never know, but I knew. I knew a lot of things. Too many things. 'When are the services?' I heard myself asking automatically.

'The day after tomorrow,' he answered. He named the chapel. 'At eleven o'clock,' he added. 'She's going to rest beside her husband and the children.'

'I'll be down,' I said. 'I'll see you there. Meanwhile, if there's anything I can do –'

'No, Brad; everything's been attended to,' he answered. 'There's nothing more anyone can do for her now.'

I put down the phone, his words ringing in my ears, and sat there staring at the papers strewn across the desk and floor. Automatically I bent to pick them up, and then suddenly the tears spilled over.

I heard the door open but I didn't look up. Mickey was standing in front of me. I felt her hand on my shoulder. 'I'm sorry, Brad,' she said.

I straightened up and looked at her. 'You know?'

She nodded. 'He told me before I put him on,' she said gently. 'It's a terrible thing.' She held out her hand. There was a drink in it.

I took the drink and held it to my lips while she picked the remaining papers from the floor. I had drained the glass by the time she had them all gathered. She looked at me questioningly.

I managed a grimace that passed for a smile. 'I'll be okay,' I said. 'Leave them here. I'll look at them later.'

She placed them in a neat stack on the desk and had started for the door when I called after her. 'No calls, Mickey, and no people. I won't be available for a while.'

She nodded, and the door shut gently behind her. I walked over to the window and looked out.

The sky was a cold winter blue and the grey white buildings of the city fought their way grimly into it. Twenty thousand square feet of earth meant half a million square feet of rental on Madison Avenue, and the new buildings were like teeming anthills all around. This was part of the big time and the big time was a part of me.

This was what I had wanted ever since I was old enough to know anything. Now I knew what it was worth. Nothing. Absolutely nothing. One tiny little person in the street was worth more than all the city put together.

She was dead but I couldn't believe it. It seemed that just a little while ago her warm lips were under mine, her voice in my ear.

Elaine. I spoke her name aloud. Before it had been a soft and loving sound but now it was a dagger in my heart. Why did you do it, Elaine?

The buzzer hawked and I went back to the desk and angrily picked up the phone. 'I thought I said no calls,' I snapped.

'Your father's here, Brad,' Mickey said softly.

'Okay,' I said and turned to face the door.

He came into the room awkwardly. Dad always looked

awkward when he walked. The only time he ever looked graceful was when he sat behind the wheel of an automobile. His dark eyes squinted searchingly up at my face. 'You heard?' he asked.

I nodded. 'Paul called me.'

'I heard it on the car radio. I came right over,' he said.

'Thanks.' I walked over to the liquor cabinet and took out a bottle. 'I'll be all right.' I poured out two drinks and held one out to him.

I swallowed mine, but he held his in his hand. 'What are you going to do?' he asked.

I shook my head. 'I don't know. When I spoke to Paul I thought I'd go down there, but now I don't know whether I can. I don't know whether I can face her.'

His eyes were still searching mine. 'Why?'

I stared at him for a moment and then I exploded. 'Why? You know as well as I, why. Because I killed her! If I had pointed a gun at her and pulled the trigger I couldn't have done a better job!' I sank into the chair beside the cabinet and put my hands over my face.

He sat down opposite me. 'How do you know?' he asked.

My eyes burned as I looked at him. 'Because I made love to her and lied to her and made promises to her that I knew I'd never keep; because she believed me and loved me and trusted me and never thought I'd leave her. When I did there was nothing left in this world for her because I had become her world.'

He sipped his drink slowly and looked at me. At last he spoke. 'You really believe that?'

I nodded.

He thought for a moment. 'Then you must go down and make your peace with her, or you'll never know another day's rest.'

'But how can I, Dad?' I cried.

He got to his feet. 'Yes, you can,' he said confidently. 'Because you're my son, Bernard. You have many of my weaknesses and all my faults, but you're not a coward. A difficult thing it may be, but you'll make your peace with her.'

The door closed behind him and I was alone again. I looked towards the window. The dark of winter had already begun to taint the day. It was not so long ago on a day like this that I first met her.

Somehow in the time between then and now I would find the answer.

Chapter ONE

I watched her in the corner of the mirror while I was shaving. The bathroom door was open and I could see her sitting up in bed. Her long reddish-brown hair cascaded over the slim white shoulders peeping from her night-dress. She wore well, I thought proudly. No one looking at her would imagine that in another three weeks we'd be married twenty years.

Twenty years. Two children – a boy nineteen, and a girl sixteen – yet she still looked like a kid herself. She was slim, small-boned and still wore the same size twelve that she did when we were first married. Her grey eyes were just as wide and bright and fresh as then and her mouth soft and full. Even without lipstick her mouth was good. It was warm and fresh and wholesome and her chin was round, yet slightly square and honest.

I saw her get out of bed and slip into a robe. Her figure was the same as it had always been, pertly, young and exciting. I watched her move out of range of the mirror and then turned back to serious shaving. I rubbed my fingers over my beard.

Still rough. It was always like that. I had to go over my beard twice before my skin would feel smooth. I picked up the shaving brush and began to re-lather my face. Suddenly I realised I was humming.

I stared in the mirror at myself in surprise. I don't ordinarily hum while shaving. I'm not usually happy at all while shaving because I hate it. If I had my way I would grow a thick black beard.

Marge always laughed at me when I complained about shaving. 'Why don't you get a job digging ditches?' she would say. 'You've got the build for it.'

I had the face for it too. One thing convinced me that you couldn't tell what a person did for a living from his appearance. Mine was one of those big rough faces that you usually associate with an outdoor, hard-working guy, but I couldn't remember the last time I did any work outside. I wouldn't even lift a finger to help out in the garden.

I began to shave again, still humming half under my breath. I was happy – why fight it? Those things were even more wonderful if they could happen to a man after twenty years of marriage.

I splashed some bay rum on my face, rinsed off the

razor and began to comb my hair. That was one point in my favour. I still had a good head of hair, even though it had gone half grey in the last five years.

The bedroom was empty when I walked back into it, but there was a clean shirt, tie, socks, underwear and a suit spread out on my bed. I grinned to myself. Marge didn't take any chances on my taste. I ran to loud combinations, but she said that didn't go with the kind of business I was in. I had to look dignified.

It hadn't always been like that. Only the last eight or nine years. Before that I could have worn a horse blanket and got away with it. But I wasn't just a press agent any more. Now I was a public relations counsellor, with thirty grand a year instead of three, and an office in one of the new buildings on Madison Avenue instead of desk space in one the size of a phone booth.

Still, when I looked in the mirror after I was dressed I had to admit to myself that Marge was right. The old boy looked solid. The clothes did something for me. They softened the harshness of my face and added a good dependable look.

When I came down to the breakfast nook, Marge was already seated at the table, reading a letter. I went over to her and kissed her cheek. 'Morning, babe,' I said.

'Morning, Brad,' she said, without taking her eyes from the letter.

I looked down over her shoulder at it. It was in a familiar hand. 'Brad?' I asked. That meant Brad Rowan, Jr. He was in his first year at college and was gone just long enough for his letters to come once a week instead of every day.

She nodded.

I walked around the table to my place and sat down. 'What's he say?' I asked, lifting my glass of orange juice.

Her grey eyes looked up at me clearly from the letter. 'He got through his exams with an eighty average. Maths was the only thing that gave him any trouble.'

I grinned at her. 'That's nothing to worry about. That would have bothered me too, if I had gone to college.' I finished the orange juice just as Sally, our maid, brought in my bacon and eggs.

Two things I especially liked. Eggs for breakfast and showers in the morning. Both were luxuries I hadn't had when I was a kid. My old man pushed a hack in New York City for a living; he still did, despite his sixty-four years. We'd never had very much. The only thing he had let me do for him was buy him his own cab. He was a peculiar old guy in many ways. Wouldn't come to live with us after Mamma passed away. 'Wouldn't feel right, away from Third Avenue El,' he said.

It was more than that, though. He didn't want to move away from Mamma. There would always be something of her around in that long railroad flat on Third Avenue. I knew how he felt, so we let it go at that.

'What else did the kid have to say?' I asked. Somehow I thought college boys were always supposed to be writing home for dough and I was secretly disappointed that Brad had never asked for any extra.

Now her eyes were troubled when she looked at me. She tapped the letter with a finger as she spoke. 'At the bottom he said he was trying to shake a cold that he had for a week since the exams but that he couldn't seem to get rid of the cough.' Her voice was worried.

I smiled at her. 'He'll be okay,' I reassured her. 'Write and tell him to go to a doctor out there.'

'He won't do it, Brad,' she protested. 'You know how he is.'

'Sure,' I answered between mouthfuls. 'All kids are

14

like that. But a cold is nothing. He'll shake it anyway. He's a husky kid.'

Just then Jeanie came into the breakfast nook. As usual she was in a hurry. 'You finished breakfast yet, Dad?' she asked.

I looked at her, smiling. Jeanie was my girl. She was the youngest. She was just like her mother, only spoiled. 'Where's the fire?' I asked. 'I gotta have my coffee.'

'But, Dad, I'll be late for school!' she protested.

I looked at her fondly. She was spoiled as hell and I'd done it all myself. 'The buses were running all morning,' I told her. 'You didn't have to wait for me.'

She put her hand on my arm and kissed my cheek. There's something about the kiss a sixteen-year-old gives her father. Sells like nothing else in the world. 'But, gee, Dad,' she said, 'you know how I like to go down to school with you.'

I grinned even though I knew she was conning me. I couldn't help it. I liked it. 'The only reason you wait for me is because I let you drive down,' I kidded her.

'Don't forget that I like your new convertible too, Dad,' she sassed me, her brown eyes laughing.

I looked over at Marge. She was watching us with a quiet smile on her lips. She knew what was going on. 'What am I gonna do with this girl?' I asked in pretended helplessness.

The quiet smile was still on her lips as she answered. 'Too late to do what you should have done,' she laughed. 'Now you might as well take her down.'

I emptied my coffee cup and got to my feet. 'Okay,' I said.

Jeanie grinned up at me. 'I'll get your hat and coat, Dad.' I could hear her running out into the foyer.

'Coming home early tonight, Brad?'

I turned back to Marge. 'I dunno yet,' I answered. 'I may get stuck with Chris on that Steel Institute deal, but I'm sure as hell gonna try.'

She got up and walked around the table towards me. I bent and kissed her cheek. It was soft and smooth. She turned her lips towards me. I kissed them. They tasted good.

'Don't work too hard, mister,' she smiled softly.

'I won't, ma'am,' I said. I heard the horn blowing out in front of the house. Jeanie had pulled the car out already. I turned and started for the door. Suddenly I stopped and looked back at her.

She was smiling after me.

I looked at her for a moment, and then I smiled. 'You know, ma'am,' I said quickly, 'if I were twenty years younger, I might marry up with you.'

Chapter TWO

October was dying all around me as I went down the walk towards the car. I was almost sorry to see it going. It was my time of year. Some like it green, but I'd take the red and brown and gold of early fall any time. The colours did something for me. It made me feel rich, warm and alive.

I stopped beside the car and stared at Jeanie. She was smiling at me. 'What are you doing with the top down?'

I asked her, picking my topcoat up from the seat beside her and shrugging myself into it.

'Gee, Dad,' she protested quickly. 'What's a convertible if you don't put the top down?'

'But, honey,' I said, clambering into the seat beside her. 'It's fall; the summer's gone already.'

She put the car into gear and we were rolling down the driveway before she answered. Then her tone was matter-of-fact. It had all the patient tolerance of the very young for the very old. 'Don't be an old fuddy-duddy, Dad,' she said plainly.

I almost smiled to myself at that. I looked over at her. She was driving with the curious concentration of hers. I saw the pink tip of her tongue peeping out from her mouth as she swung out of the driveway into the street. The curve of the driveway always made her do that.

I felt the car pick up speed as she pressed down on the accelerator. I glanced over at the speedometer. We were hitting forty in less than a block and the needle was still climbing. 'Use a light foot, honey,' I cautioned.

Her eyes glanced away from the road at me for a moment. They told me more than anything she could say. I even began to feel old. I shut up guiltily and looked at the road ahead.

In a few seconds I began to feel better. She was right. What good was a convertible if the top wasn't down? There's something about riding down a country road in the early fall with the open sky above you and the flaming colours all around.

Her voice took me by surprise. 'What are you getting Mother for your anniversary, Dad?'

I looked at her. Her eyes were still on the road. I stumbled a little over my answer. I hadn't thought about it. 'I don't know,' I confessed.

Her eyes flashed over me quickly. 'Don't you think you'd better decide?' she said practically in that way women have when talking about gifts. 'It's less than four weeks away.'

'Yeah,' I mumbled. 'I better think of something.' I had an idea. 'Maybe you know what she'd like?'

She shook her head. 'Uh-uh, not me. That's your headache. I was just wondering.'

'What made you wonder?' I asked, suddenly curious about what went on in that pretty little head.

She stopped the car for a traffic light and looked over at me. 'No special reason,' she smiled slowly. 'I was just wondering if you were going to come home with the usual last-minute bouquet.'

I could feel my face blush. I hadn't realised those young eyes could see so much. 'I never really know what to get her.'

Her eyes were on my face. 'You have absolutely no imagination, have you, Dad?' she asked.

I began to feel flustered. 'Wait a minute, Jeanie,' I said. 'I'm a pretty busy guy. I can't think of everything. Besides, your Mother has everything she wants. What else can I get her?'

She put the car into gear again and we began to roll. 'Sure, Dad,' she said, a certain dryness in her tone. 'Mother has everything she wants. A new refrigerator, stove, washing machine.' Her eyes swung back to me. 'Did you ever think of getting her something for herself? Something not quite so useful, but that she would get a kick out of having?'

I was beginning to feel desperate. She had something up her sleeve. 'Like what, for instance?'

'A mink coat, for instance,' she said quickly, her eyes on the road ahead.

I stared at her. 'Is that what she wants?' I asked almost incredulously. 'She always said she didn't want a mink coat.'

'Daddy, you're such a dope. What woman wouldn't like a mink coat, no matter what they say?' She was laughing at me now. 'Honest, I don't know what Mother saw in you. You're not the least bit romantic.'

In spite of myself I began to smile. For a moment I felt like asking her if she still thought the stork had brought her, but you just can't talk like that to a sixteen-year-old who knows everything, even if she is your daughter. I spoke seriously. 'You think I ought to get her a mink coat?'

She nodded her head as she came to a stop across the way from the school.

'Then I'll do it,' I said.

'You're not really so bad, Dad,' she said, leaning against the door as she closed it.

I slid over behind the wheel and put my face very close to her. 'Thanks,' I said solemnly.

She kissed my cheek quickly. 'Bye now, Dad.'

I got into the office about eleven. I was feeling pretty good. Don had told me that he would really do something special for her. He had her measurements from the Persian she had ordered last summer. I was sure he'd do all right. He'd better. Sixty-five hundred clams for a mink coat didn't come off trees.

Mickey looked up at me as I came in. 'Where have you been, boss?' she asked, taking my hat and coat. 'Paul Remey's been calling you from Washington all morning.'

'Shopping,' I said. I walked into my office. She followed me. I turned around. 'What's he want?'

'He didn't say,' she answered. 'Only that he had to speak to you right away.'

'Call him back then,' I told her, sitting down behind my desk. The door closed behind her as I wondered what Paul wanted. I hoped everything was all right with him. You could never tell in a political job, though, no matter how good you were – even if you were a special Presidential assistant as Paul was.

I really liked the guy. If it weren't for him I would never be where I was today. In a way he was responsible for it. It went all the way back to the early days of the war.

I had been enthusiastically rejected by all branches of the armed services and finally wound up in the publicity division of the War Production Board. That's where I first met Paul. He was the chief in charge of a section devoted to building up the scrap drive and I was assigned to his office.

It was one of those things. Two guys cotton to each other right away. He had been a very successful business-man out West and sold out his business to come to Washington for a dollar a year. I had been working for a picture company and came to Washington because I heard the pickings were good and I had just been canned by the outfit I worked for.

He did a hell of a job, and he thought I did too. When the war ended he called me into his office. 'What're you going to do now, Brad?' he asked.

I remember shrugging my shoulders. 'Look for a job, I guess,' I had answered.

'Did you ever think about going into business for your-self?' he had asked.

I'd shrugged. 'That's a big-time operation,' I replied. 'I can't afford it. I ain't got the dough.'

'I don't mean that,' he had said. 'I mean public relations. I happen to know a few businessmen who might be interested in the kind of help you can give them. You'd need only a small place to get started.'

I had looked down across his desk at him. 'This is a press agent's pipe dream,' I had said, sliding into the chair opposite him. 'But keep on talking to me. Don't stop.'

That was the beginning. It led to a small one-room office with Mickey, my secretary, then to the large offices we had now with more than twenty-five people working. Paul had many friends, and his friends had many friends.

The phone buzzer rang and I reached for the receiver. Mickey's voice was in my ear. 'Mr Remey's on the phone, Brad.'

I pressed down the through button. 'Hello, Paul,' I said. 'How's things?'

I could hear Paul's warm chuckle, and then his favourite profanity. 'They'll never improve, Brad,' he finished.

'Don't give up hope, boss,' I assured him. 'You never can tell.'

He laughed again, then his voice came through the phone seriously. 'I was wondering if you could do me a favour, Brad?'

'Anything, Paul,' I answered. 'Just ask me.'

'It's one of those charity things of Edith's again,' he said.

Edith was his wife. A sweet woman, but she'd got a taste of the D.C. whirlpool and it went to her head. I had helped out on some of her projects before. It was one of those things you had to do but I didn't mind as long as it was for Paul. He did enough for me. 'Sure, Paul,' I said quickly. 'I'll be glad to. Just shoot me the dope.'

'I don't know very much about it, Brad,' he answered.

'All I know is that Edith told me to be sure and call you and tell you that a Mrs Hortense E. Schuyler will be in to see you this afternoon and give you all the information.'

'Okay, Paul,' I said, scribbling down the name. 'I'll take care of things.'

'And Brad,' Paul said, 'Edith cautioned me to tell you to be especially nice to the girl. She says it means a lot to her.'

I liked the way Edith used the word girl. Edith was in her middle fifties, and all her friends were girls to her. 'Tell Edith not to worry,' I said. 'I'll give her the A treatment.'

He laughed. 'Thanks, Brad. You know what these things mean to Edith.'

'I know,' I answered. 'You can count on me.'

We spoke a few more words and I hung up the phone. I looked down at the scratch paper. Hortense E. Schuyler. All those dames in Washington had names like that. And they looked like it too. I pressed the buzzer.

Mickey came into the office, her pad and pencil in hand. 'Let's go to work,' I said. 'You've wasted enough time around here this morning.'

Chapter THREE

It was about four-thirty in the afternoon and Chris and I were just getting down to cost factors on institutional steel copy when the intercom's buzz called me from the wallboard. I walked quickly to my desk and flipped the switch.

'No calls, Mickey,' I said, annoyance in my voice. 'I told you before.' I closed the switch and walked back to wallboard. 'So gimme the figures, Chris.'

His pale blue eyes glittered behind the wide steel rimmed glasses. He looked almost happy. He always looked happy when he spoke about money. 'Once a week in four hundred papers,' he said in his nasal, precise voice, 'will come to five hundred and fifteen thousand dollars. One fifteen per cent placement on that amounts to seventy-seven thousand. Art work, copy and make-up charges will be a thousand a week, fifty-two thousand for the year.'

'Great, great,' I said interrupting him patiently. 'But can we handle it? I don't want to find myself in the wrong boat like on that Mason job last year.'

He looked at me calmly. I had taken a job for thirty-five grand that cost us sixty to deliver. He smiled coldly. 'That's what you pay me for,' he pointed out. 'To keep you from making mistakes like that again.'

I nodded my head. 'How much?'

'Cost you four hundred a week,' he said. 'We come out a hundred and eight thousand ahead.'

I smiled at him. 'Good boy,' I said, clapping him on the shoulder. 'Now let's take a look at the campaign.'

He permitted himself the vestige of a smile before he turned back to the wallboard on which the first series of ads were placed. There were ten advertisements resting there, all very neat in their grey cardboard mountings.

I heard the door open behind us. I turned around. Mickey was coming towards me. 'I thought I said I didn't want to be bothered,' I snapped.

'Mrs Schuyler is here to see you, Brad,' she said calmly, ignoring my ill temper.

I stared at her blankly. 'Mrs Schuyler? Who the hell is she?'

Mickey looked down at a small calling card she held in her hand. 'Mrs Hortense E. Schuyler,' she read from it.

She held it out towards me. 'She says she has an appointment with you.'

I took the card from her hand and looked at it. Just the name in simple type. It rang no bells. I gave it back to her. 'I don't remember any appointment,' I said. 'I purposely kept all afternoon open so Chris and I could get through this job.'

There was a peculiar look in Mickey's eyes as she took the card from me. 'What shall I tell her?' she asked.

I shrugged my shoulders. 'Tell her anything. I went out of town or I'm in conference. Only get rid of her. I want to finish this.' I had already turned back to the wallboard.

Mickey's voice came over my shoulder. 'She says she'll understand if you can't see her because of the short notice. But she's due back in Washington tomorrow afternoon and would like to know what would be a convenient time.'

That did it. Now I remembered. This was one of Edith Remey's 'girls'. I turned around quickly. 'Why didn't you say so the first time?' I asked. 'That's why Paul called me this morning. I gotta see her.' I thought. 'Hold her for a few minutes. Make some apology for my delay and I'll call you as soon as I'm through.'

The peculiar look faded from Mickey's eyes and something like relief came into them. 'Okay, boss,' she snapped smartly, turning on her heel and walking out of the office.

I looked at Chris. 'Well, that does it,' I said disgustedly. 'We'll have to take the rest of this up in the morning.'

'It doesn't give you much time to absorb the plan before you see Matt Brady and the committee at two,' he said.

I started walking back to my desk. 'Can't help it, Chris,' I called back over my shoulder. 'If I get stuck I'll just have to fake it. I've done that before.'

He was standing in front of my desk, a look of disapproval on his face. 'These boys are sharp, though.'

I sat down and looked at him. 'Stop worrying, Chris,' I told him. 'They're human, ain't they? The same as us. They like money, dames, liquor. They wear clothes, not wings. We'll get to them the same way as we get to anybody else. Everybody can be reached once you know what they're looking for. And when we find out, we'll get the job. It's as easy as that.'

He was shaking his head as I flipped the intercom switch. I half laughed to myself. Poor old Chris. He still lived in an old-fashioned world where business was just that and no more. I remembered the first time he had heard me get a dame for a customer. He had turned so red I thought the colour would rub off on his starched white collar. 'Okay, Mickey,' I said into the intercom. 'Send the old bag in.'

Through the speaker I could hear a sudden swift intake of breath. 'What did you say, Brad?' her voice echoed incredulously in my ear.

'I said send the old bag in. What's the matter with you this afternoon? You deaf or something?'

Her whisper was almost a chuckle. 'You never saw her before?'

'No,' I snapped. 'And after today, I hope I'll never have to again.'

She was really laughing now. 'Ten to one you change your mind. If you don't, I'll really believe you the next time you tell me you gave up women.'

The intercom clicked off and I looked up at Chris. 'She's gone nuts,' I told him.

He smiled bleakly and started for the door. Before he got there it started to open. He stepped quickly to one side so that it could swing past him.

I could hear Mickey's voice. 'Right this way, Mrs Schuyler.'

I started slowly to get to my feet as Mickey came through the door. Chris was staring past her into the outer office. There was a look on his face I had never seen before.

Then she came in, and I knew what the look on his face meant. The guy didn't have dollar bills running through his veins, after all.

The expression on my face must have been worth the price of admission, for Mickey was smiling as she closed the door behind Chris and herself. I found myself walking unsteadily around my desk towards her. 'Mrs Schuyler,' I said, holding out my hand. 'I'm Brad Rowan.'

She smiled at me, taking my hand. 'I'm glad to meet you, Mr Rowan,' she said softly. 'Edith told me so much about you.' Her voice sounded like chimes ringing in the office.

I looked at her. I'd seen dames before. Lots of them. When I worked for a movie company I squired some of the most beautiful dames in the world around. It was my job. They didn't bother me. I could take 'em and leave 'em. But this one was something special.

This one was class. Blue chip stocks on the big board. The gold standard. Big white orchids in florists' windows. A Rodgers and Hammerstein score. A lazy sun in the summer morning. The green, friendly earth. Ruby port after dinner. A Billy Eckstine love chant.

Her hair was a rich soft brown, short in the front, long in the back, almost to her shoulders. Her eyes were dark blue almost violet, with large black pupils that you could almost dive into. Her face was not quite round, her cheekbones high, her mouth soft and generous, her chin not quite square, her nose not quite tilted, her teeth white

29

and even, not dentist's even but human even.

I drew a deep breath and sucked in my gut. Suddenly I wished I had got in a little more tennis or golf last summer so that the slight paunch I was developing would not show. 'Make it Brad,' I smiled, pulling out a chair for her. 'Please sit down.'

She sat down, and still in a sort of daze I went back behind my big desk to recuperate.

I looked over at her. She was slipping off her gloves and I could see her hands, white and slim and small-boned with a slight coral polish on the nails. She wore one large white diamond on her left hand, no other ring.

'Paul told me you were coming in,' I said awkwardly. 'But I hadn't expected you so soon. What can I do for you, Mrs Schuyler?'

She smiled again. It was like there were no other lights in the room. 'Make it Elaine,' she said.

'Eh-laine,' I said after her, saying it as she did.

She smiled again. 'I never liked Hortense.' Her voice was gently confidential. 'I never forgave Mother for that.'

I grinned. 'I know just what you mean. I was christened Bernard. Everybody called me Bernie.'

She took a cigarette from a flat golden case and I almost broke my neck getting around the desk to light it for her. She drew on it deeply and let out the smoke slowly.

I went back to my chair and sat down. I was still arguing with myself. I couldn't understand it.

Her eyes were wide as she looked at me. 'Edith told me to look you up, because' – she laughed gently – 'you were the only man in the world who could help me.'

I let myself laugh with her. I began to feel better. My control was coming back. I was on ground I could understand now. The old build-up. I looked at her again. I guess what got me was that I had expected somebody else. I never thought Edith's girls could be anything but carbons of Edith herself. 'How?' I asked.

'I've been appointed chairman of our local committee on the Infantile drive and I thought you might be able to help me plan a campaign that would really produce results.' She looked at me expectantly.

I could feel a tough cynicism creeping back into my joints. She was one of Edith's girls, after all, no matter what she looked like. The only thing that was important to her was that she would get enough space in the papers to compensate her for her effort. I felt disappointment.

Didn't know why I should, but I did anyway. These society dames were all alike. Class or no class, they were like any publicity hungry dame, looking for some fat clippings. I got to my feet.

'I'll be very glad to help, Mrs Schuyler,' I said brusquely. 'If you'd leave your name and address with my secretary and keep her informed of any activities on the part of your organisation or yourself, we will see to it that you get proper publicity and coverage.'

She was staring up at me in some sort of surprise. Her eyes expressed a bewilderment at the sudden manner in which our talk had ended. Her voice was lightly incredulous. 'Is that all you can do, Mr Rowan?'

I stared back at her in irritation. I was getting sick and tired of all the phonies who wore mink to their committee meetings. 'Isn't that what you want, Mrs Schuyler?' I asked nastily. 'After all, we can't give you a written guarantee on the space we can grab for you, but we'll get our share. Isn't that what you're in this for?'

Her mouth closed suddenly. Her eyes got dark and cold. Silently she got to her feet, tapping her cigarette out in the tray beside the chair. She picked her pocket-book up from the chair and when she turned back to me her face was as grim and cold as her eyes. The tone of her voice went mine one better. 'You misunderstand me, Mr Rowan. I'm not looking for any personal publicity out of this. I've had more than enough of it. The only reason I came to see you was to work out a campaign for the Infantile drive next January. The only reason I accepted the job was because I know what it means to lose some-one to that dreadful disease and I don't want any other wife or mother to go through what I did.' She turned and started for the door.

I stared after her in confusion for a moment. Then a glimpse of her profile set in white anger did it and I remembered. Her name escaped my lips. 'Mrs David E. Schuyler!' Now I knew the whole story. Silently I cursed myself for a fool. The papers had been full of her last year. How she had lost her twin children and her husband to infantile.

I caught her at the door just before she opened it. I leaned against it, holding it closed. She looked up at me. I could see the faint trace of angry tears in her eyes.

'Mrs Schuyler,' I said contritely. 'Could you forgive a stupid Third Avenue mug who thinks he knows every-thing? I'm really ashamed.'

Her eyes looked deep into mine for a long moment, then she drew a deep breath and silently walked back to the chair. She took out her cigarette case and opened it. I could see her fingers trembling as she put the cigarette in her mouth. I held a match for her.

'I'm very sorry,' I said as the flame flared golden on her face. 'I thought you were just another one of those women who were looking for glory.'

Her eyes were still staring up into mine and I could see the smoke curling blue around her face. Then there was nothing but her eyes and I was lost in the whirling dark blue pain of them. I fought an impulse to take her in my arms and wash the pain away. No one should know such pain.

Her voice was very still and gentle. 'If you'll really help me, Brad, I'll forgive you.'

Chapter FOUR

The phone buzzed. It was Chris. 'The accountant just verified last month's net,' he said.

I looked over at Elaine. 'Excuse me a moment,' I smiled. 'Business.'

'Of course,' she nodded.

'Okay, shoot,' I said into the phone.

'Profit before taxes, twenty-one thousand; after taxes, nine,' he said in his dull, dry voice.

'Good,' I said into the phone. 'Go down the line.'

'Have you the time?' he asked, a faint touch of sarcasm in his voice.

'I got the time,' I said coldly.

He began reeling off a string of figures from the profit and loss balance sheets. I paid no attention to them. I was watching her.

She had left her chair and walked over to the wall and was examining the steel layouts. I liked the way she moved, the way she held herself, the way she cocked her head on one side to study a drawing. She must have felt my gaze on her back for suddenly she turned around and smiled at me.

I returned her smile and she came back to the desk and sat down. At last he was finished and I put down the phone. 'I'm sorry,' I said.

'Don't apologise,' she said. 'I understand.' She looked at the drawings on the wallboard. 'They seem like rather unusual ads. They don't sell anything specific. Only the functions of steel.'

'That's what they're supposed to do,' I said. 'That's part of a special campaign we're whipping up for the American Steel Institute.'

'Oh, the institutional public relations campaign?' she exclaimed.

'You know about it?'

'That's all I've been hearing about the last two weeks,' she said. I looked puzzled and she explained. 'My uncle Matthew Brady, is chairman of the board of Consolidated Steel. I've just come from two weeks at his house.'

I let out a whistle. Matt Brady was the last of the old-line steel men. A pirate down to his fingertips. Sharp, cold, ruthless. I had heard he was the nut we have to crack to get anywhere, and he was the guy Chris had been afraid of.

She began to laugh. 'You've got such a funny expression on your face. What are you thinking?'

I searched her eyes for a moment and decided this was a dame to be honest with. 'I was just thinking that a kind fate must have been watching over me. I might've chased you out of my office. And Matt Brady your uncle. That would have been the end of my crack at the steel account.'

'Do you think that would have made any difference to me?' she asked, the laughter fading from her face.

'Uh-uh,' I shook my head. 'Not to you. But it would to me if I were your uncle. If I were Matt Brady, nobody would dare treat you mean.'

The laughter came back to her eyes. 'Then you don't know my uncle,' she said. 'When it comes to business, personal relationships don't mean a thing to him.'

'That's what I heard,' I said. I heard worse than that but I didn't tell her.

'But he's sweet, and I'm very fond of him,' she added quickly.

I smiled to myself at that. It was pretty hard to picture Matt Brady as a sweet character. Matt Brady, who had pushed all the small steel companies up against the wall during the last depression and then took them over for a song. God only knew how many people he had broken with that simple altruistic gesture.

I looked down at our notes. 'Enough of that,' I said. 'To get back to our own problems. The trouble with any of these drives is that the public is sick and tired of hard luck stories and doesn't want to hear any more of them. But I think we can lick that if you have the guts.'

Her mouth tightened. 'I'll do anything to help.'

'Good,' I said. 'Then we'll set up a whole batch of newspaper, radio, and TV interviews for you. You'll tell them your own story. Simply. Personally.'

A shadow fell across her eyes. I never saw a face with so much pain in it. Impulsively I reached for her hand. It lay still and quiet in mine. 'You don't have to,' I said quickly, wanting to take that hurt. 'There are other ways. We'll find them.'

Quietly she withdrew her hand from mine and clasped them in her lap. Her eyes were steady. 'We'll do it,' she said. 'You're right. It's the best way.'

She had guts, real guts. Matt Brady's niece was nothing he'd need to be ashamed of. 'Good girl,' I said.

The intercom buzzed and I flipped the switch. 'Yes?'

Mickey's voice came through, flat and metallic. 'It's six-thirty, boss, and I've got a heavy date tonight. Do you want me to hang around?'

I looked at my watch and cursed. I hadn't realised it was that late. 'Go ahead, Mickey,' I told her. 'I'll wrap up.'

'Thanks, boss,' her voice came back. 'You can leave the tenner on my desk. Good night.'

I closed the switch and turned to Elaine. She was smiling at me.

'I didn't mean to keep you so late, Brad,' she said.

'Nor I you,' I told her.

'But you'll be late getting home for dinner, while my time is my own,' she pointed out.

'Marge won't mind,' I answered quickly. 'She's used to it.'

She walked over to where her handbag lay. 'Nevertheless I'd better be going,' she said, taking out a long slim tube of lipstick and beginning to apply it.

I watched her. 'But we haven't nearly finished yet,' I said, a curious reluctance in me to see her getting ready to leave. 'And you're going back to Washington tomorrow.'

She glanced over the top of her mirror at me. 'But I'll be back next week.' She checked the lipstick line and began to close the tube. 'We can pick up then.'

'Things are never as good when you have to come back and pick them up again,' I heard myself saying.

Her eyes were fixed on me speculatively. 'Then what do you suggest?' she asked.

I was being more surprised at myself every moment. 'Let's stay down and have dinner, if you have no other engagement,' I said quickly. 'Then we can come back here and finish up.'

Her eyes looked into mine for a moment then almost imperceptibly she shook her head. 'We'd better not,' she said. 'I won't feel right in upsetting your evening. Bad enough I had to bother you as it is.'

I went over and helped her into her fur jacket. 'Okay,' I said, disappointment showing in my voice. 'How about a drink, then?'

She turned around and looked at me squarely. 'What are you looking for, Brad?'

The surprise on my face wasn't quite genuine. 'I'm not looking for anything. Do you have to look for something if you want to buy a woman a drink?'

Her face was unsmiling. 'Not necessarily. But you didn't impress me as the kind of man who goes around buying drinks for women.'

I could feel a flush creeping into my face. 'I'm not.'

Her eyes were still trying to read my face. 'Then why me?'

I felt awkward and embarrassed, like a kid who asked a girl for a date and was turned down flat. I found what seemed like a good answer. 'Because I'm sorry about how I acted when you first came in, and I want to prove it to you.'

Her face relaxed and some of the tension went out of it. 'You don't have to do that, Brad,' she said quietly. 'You've already proved that.'

I didn't answer.

'Good night, Brad,' she said, holding out her hand, 'and thanks.'

I took her hand. It was small and light and the skin was smooth in my fingers. I looked down at it for a moment and her coral nail polish gleamed up at me. I smiled. 'Good night, Elaine.'

'I'll be back in town Monday and we can get together then, if it's convenient for you,' she said:

'Any time you say,' I said, still holding her hand. I could feel a pulse racing in my temples.

She looked down at her hand and withdrew it gently. I could see her face flush. She turned and started for the door.

'If you're in town early enough,' I called after her, 'let's make lunch.'

She stopped and looked back at me. 'Where?'

I rested my hands on my desk behind me. 'Pick me up here about one.'

'It's a date,' she said, still not smiling.

I watched the door close behind her and walked around my desk and sat down. I stared at the door. Her perfume was still in my nostrils. I breathed deeply and it was gone. I leaned forward and picked up the phone to tell Marge I'd be home for dinner by eight.

All the way home I kept thinking about her. The more I thought about her the angrier I got with myself. What had got into me anyway? She wasn't the most beautiful dame I had ever seen in my life. Neither was she the sexiest. She wasn't stacked like that.

While we were eating dinner I told Marge all about her and the way I had acted when she came into the office.

Marge listened to me silently in that attentive way she had and when I finished, she let out a small sigh.

'What's that for?' I asked quickly.

'Poor woman,' she said slowly. 'Poor, unhappy woman.'

I stared at her as if she had just turned on the lights in a dark room and I could see again. That was it. She had hit the nail right. Elaine Schuyler meant nothing to me at all. I felt the way I did because I was sorry for her.

I began to feel better, more like myself again. That had to be the reason. By the time I went to bed I was convinced it was.

But I was wrong, and I knew it the moment she walked into my office on Monday.

Chapter FIVE

By the time I got down to the office on Monday I was back to normal. I had everything figured out. I would have lunch with her, be polite and helpful and that would be all there was to it.

I smiled as I sat down to my morning mail. What a fool I had almost made of myself. I should have known better. I was past that. Forty-three was too old.

There is a stage in a man's life where a woman is important, and sex and romance are synonymous. But that comes while you're young, not at forty-three. At forty-three you've got other things to think about. It's part of growing up and I've seen it in almost every man I know. By forty-three, sex and romance require too much effort, take too much out of you emotionally and physically. You need the drive for other things. Business, for example.

I remember hearing someone say that business was the American substitute for sex. As a man grew older and his drive weakened, he looked about for other fields in which he could demonstrate his abilities. Business was the logical out. That's why so many men made mistresses of their work. That was why so many wives were unhappy too, but that was the normal hazard of marriage. It made sense to me. And man has just so much strength, and I was smart enough to know my limitations. Besides, she was Matt Brady's niece and there was no point in looking for trouble.

By the time one o'clock rolled around I had almost forgotten about my luncheon date. It had been a hectic morning and I had created a very demanding mistress. The intercom buzzed and I pressed the key down impatiently.

'Mrs Schuyler is here.' The words lingered in my ears.

I sucked in my breath sharply. A quick excitement began to pound through me. 'Ask her to come in,' I said, getting to my feet.

I was the smart one, all right; I had everything figured out. A moment before I hadn't thought about her, she hadn't been important to me. But now she was.

I knew it as I waited for the door to open. I couldn't wait. I wanted to hurry to it and open it for her. I began to move around the desk but she had already come into the office.

I had thought it wouldn't happen again. It couldn't happen again. It had been that way the first time I saw her but it wouldn't be this time. This time I knew what she was like. I had my guard up. I was wrong about that too.

She smiled at me and I could hardly speak. 'Hello, Brad.' Her voice was low and warm.

For a moment I hesitated; then I walked across the room and took her hand. 'Elaine.' Her soft, cool fingers were like fire in my palm. 'Elaine,' I repeated. 'I'm so glad you could come.'

She started to laugh, to make some merry, inconsequential remark, but she looked up into my face and the words stopped in her throat. A shadow came into her eyes and she looked away from me.

'I'm sorry, Brad,' she almost whispered, withdrawing her hand. 'I can't make lunch with you.'

'Why not?' I blurted out.

She still didn't look up at me. 'I had forgotten a previous appointment. I just dropped by to apologise.'

I stared at her. The clear, fragile profile etched deeply into my mind. I felt a chill sweeping all the excitement out of me. I was suddenly angry. 'You're joking!' I accused flatly.

She didn't answer.

I took a step towards her. 'If you had another appointment you would have called me,' I said roughly. 'You didn't have to come up here for that. There are too many telephones in this town.'

She turned towards the door and started away from me. I could feel an angry, helpless frustration choking up in me. I seized her shoulders and turned her towards me. 'Why are you lying to me?' I demanded, staring into her face.

There was a bright shining moisture in her eyes. 'Brad, I'm not lying to you,' she answered in a small voice.

I paid no attention to her denial. 'What are you afraid of, Elaine?' I asked harshly.

I could feel her slump suddenly under my hands as if all the strength had run out of her. The tears were clear in her eyes now. 'Let me go, Brad,' she whispered. 'Haven't I had enough trouble?'

Her tiny voice spilled over me like a spray of cold water, washing away my anger. I dropped my hands and walked slowly back to my desk. I slumped into my chair. After a moment I looked up at her. 'Okay, Elaine,' I said. 'You can go if you want.'

She hesitated, looking back at me. 'Brad, I'm sorry.'

I didn't answer.

I watched the door close behind her and then looked blackly down at my desk. She was right. There was no arguing about it. I was only looking for trouble. This was no dame that you could pick up for a time and then toss away. This baby had class and the only way you could play was for keeps.

I stuck a cigarette between my lips and lit it. It was probably the best thing that could have happened. Forty-three was too old to start getting the dreams of youth.

Somehow the day crept by, and about five o'clock when the telephone rang there was nothing left inside me but the vague ache of a might-have-been. I picked up the phone.

'Paul Remey on the phone, boss,' Mickey said.

I switched over. 'Paul, how are you?' I asked.

'Fine, Brad,' he answered. 'Free for dinner tonight?'

Surprise crept into my voice. 'Sure,' I said quickly. 'Where the devil are you?'

'I'm in town,' he laughed at my surprise. 'I had to mend

a fence for the Chief. Edith came in with me to do a little shopping. I just got the bright idea of calling you for dinner. It's got to be early though. I'm getting the nine o'clock plane back.'

'Wonderful,' I said, making my voice as cordial as I could. 'Suppose we met at twenty-one six? We can take our time over dinner, and then I'll drive you out to the airport.'

'Okay,' he replied. 'See you there.'

I put down the phone and looked out the window. It was almost dark, with the surprising early dark that comes after Daylight Saving Time is over. I felt very tired. All I wanted to do was to go home and crawl into bed and sleep away the vague unsatisfied feeling inside me. But there was some things that I had to do.

I picked up the phone again and called home. Marge answered. 'I won't be home for dinner, baby,' I said. 'Paul's in town and I'm eating with him. Want to come down and join us?' I asked.

'I don't think so,' she answered. 'I'll have dinner with Jeanie and turn in early. You boys have a good time.'

'Okay, baby,' I replied. 'Bye now.'

I turned back to my desk and finished reading the estimates on the steel job. I initialled them and sent them into Chris's office. By that time it was six o'clock, so I left.

The night had turned cool and the air was crisp. I took a deep breath and decided a few blocks' walk couldn't do me any harm. I walked down Madison to Fifty-second Street, then over to the restaurant.

The maître d' caught me just as I checked my hat. 'Mr Rowan,' he smoothied. 'Mr Remey's waiting for you. Right this way, please.'

Paul got to his feet as I approached the table. Edith

was sitting to his right. After I shook his hand I turned to her and smiled. 'Edith, this is such a wonderful surprise,' I said. 'Marge will be so disappointed you didn't let us know you'd be in town.'

She smiled back at me. 'It was unexpected, Brad,' she answered. 'But it's good to see you.'

'You too,' I said, sitting down. 'You're looking younger each time.'

She laughed. 'Same old Brad,' she said. But I know she liked it.

I noticed there was a place set at the table for a fourth. I looked at Paul questioningly. 'Somebody's missing?' I asked.

He started to reply but Edith beat him to it. 'No,' she said. 'Here she comes now.'

I saw Paul glance over my shoulder and begin to rise to his feet. Automatically I followed suit. I turned around.

I think we saw each other at the same moment. A bright glow appeared in her eyes, and then as quickly disappeared. She seemed to hesitate for a moment, then continued on towards the table.

She held out her hand. 'Mr Rowan,' she said in a politely formal voice. 'It's good to see you again.'

I took her hand. Her fingers were trembling excitedly in mine. I held her chair while she sat down. Edith leaned forward, smiling. 'At the last minute Elaine met me for lunch and went shopping with me, Brad. She has such wonderful taste. We bought out half the stores in New York.'

'I hope you left me with enough money to pay for dinner,' Paul joked.

Edith said something to him, but I didn't hear her reply. I couldn't tell if the building were to collapse around me.

I was looking at Elaine and her eyes were a smoky blue and hurt. Her mouth was soft and red and warm. And all I could think about was how wonderful it would be to kiss her.

Chapter SIX

At eight, while we were dawdling over coffee, the captain came over to the table. 'Your car is outside, Mr Rowan,' he informed me.

'Thanks,' I replied. I had called the garage before I left the office and told them to deliver the car by eight. I looked around the table. 'Ready?'

'Ready,' Paul answered.

Edith whipped out her compact and put the face through a last-minute fix while I turned to Elaine.

'How about joining us for a ride out to the airport?' I asked.

She shook her head. 'I think I'd better turn in. I'm tired. Thank you just the same, Mr Rowan.'

'Oh, Elaine, come on,' Edith said. 'Brad will drop you back at the hotel by ten. A little fresh air won't hurt you.'

Elaine looked at me, hesitating.

I nodded. 'We can be back in town by ten,' I said.

'Okay.' She smiled, 'I'll go with you.'

On the way out, the women sat together in the back while Paul and I sat in the front seat. Every now and then I would look up into the rear-view mirror and she would be watching me. She would turn her eyes away quickly, but then when I would look again, her eyes would have returned.

I told him about the difficulties involved in the steel account and he told me all the latest gossip around Washington. The drive passed quickly and we arrived at the airport at ten minutes to nine. I parked the car and we all walked over to the gate. We exchanged good-byes and I promised to have Marge call Edith tomorrow. Then Paul and Edith walked through the gate and Elaine and I went back to the car.

We didn't speak. I held the door open for her silently while she got in, then walked around the other side and got in behind the wheel. I reached forward to turn on the ignition, but her hand stopped me.

'Wait a minute,' she said. 'Till their plane takes off.'

I leaned back in the seat and looked at her. She was looking through the windshield at the plane. There was a lonely look on her face.

'Is there anything wrong?' I asked quickly.

She shook her head. 'No,' she answered. 'I just want to see them off safely.'

'You think a lot of them?' I said. It was more a statement than a question.

She nodded. 'I love them,' she said simply. 'I don't know how I would have managed after what happened if it hadn't been for Edith and Paul.'

I lit a cigarette just as the plane motors split the night. We were silent until the plane had roared into the darkness. Then she turned to me.

There was a half smile on her lips. 'Okay now.'

I didn't move. I watched her face in the glow of the cigarette. Her skin was a creamy gold and there were flecks of fire deep in her eyes.

She was looking at me too, the smile gone from her lips. 'I never expected to see you again,' she whispered.

'Nor I, you,' I replied. 'Are you sorry?'

She thought for a moment. 'There's really no answer, Brad,' she said, 'I don't know how I feel.'

'I know how I feel,' I said surely.

'That's different,' she said quickly. 'You're a man. You feel differently about things. Nothing is as important to a man as it is to a woman.'

'Isn't it?' I asked. I flipped the cigarette out the window and put my hands on her shoulders and drew her towards me. I kissed her.

Her lips did not move, yet were not still; they were not cold but neither were they warm; they did not kiss back, and still they made love to me.

I raised my lips from hers and looked at her face. Her eyes were wide open gazing into mine.

'I wanted to kiss you from the first moment I saw you,' I said.

She drew back to her side of the car and took out a cigarette. I held a match for her. She drew deeply on her cigarette and leaned her head back against the cushion.

She didn't look at me. 'When David was alive, I would not look at another man, nor he at another woman.'

Her eyes were sombre and thoughtful as I watched her. I didn't speak.

'During the war,' she continued, almost reflectively, 'we were separated a great deal. You know what Washington was like then. You were there. Everybody was on the make. Nothing seemed to matter. It used to make me sick.'

I still watched her silently.

'It still does,' she said slowly. She looked directly at me and her face was carefully impassive.

I met her gaze evenly. Our eyes met and locked in silent conflict, 'Are you still in love with your husband?' I asked.

Her eyelashes swept low over her eyes, hiding them from me. There was a quiet pain in her voice. 'That's not a fair question. David is dead.'

'But you're not,' I pointed out cruelly. 'You're a grown woman now, not a child any longer. You have needs – '

'Men?' she asked, interrupting me. 'Sex?' She laughed thinly. 'You think that's important?'

'Love is important,' I answered. 'Loving and being loved is necessary to everyone.'

Her eyes came up again to mine. 'Are you saying that you're in love with me?' she asked sceptically.

I thought for a moment. 'I don't know,' I answered slowly. 'I might be, but I don't know.'

'What are you trying to say then, Brad?' she asked. 'Why aren't you honest with me – with yourself – and say what you really want?'

I looked down at my hands to escape the pull in her glance. 'Right now, all I know is that I want you,' I said. She was silent and when I looked up at her, the cigarette

was burning, forgotten in her fingers. 'From the moment
I first saw you, I wanted you. I don't know what it is, or
how or why. But I knew I wanted you more than anything I ever wanted in my whole life.' I reached for her
hand.

Her face was very still. 'Brad,' she said quietly.

I bent my face towards her and kissed her lips. This
time they were not still and were not cold. They were
soft and sweet and trembling. My arms went around her
and we drew closer together and our kiss lasted until we
ran out of breath.

She rested her head on my arm across the seat behind
her. Her eyes looked up at me gently. They were fond
and rich and warm. 'Brad,' she whispered.

I kissed her again quickly. 'Yes, Elaine?'

Her lips moved softly under mine. 'Let's not be like all
the others, Brad. Don't do anything you'll regret.'

'Up to now,' I said quickly, 'all you talked about is me.
What about you? What do you want?'

'What I want is not as important as you, Brad,' she
answered quietly. 'You have more to lose than I.'

I didn't answer. There was nothing I could say.

Again she looked into my eyes. 'How do you feel
about your wife, Brad? Do you love her?'

'Of course I love her,' I said quickly. Then as the
words echoed inadequately in the air, I added, 'You
don't stay married for as long as we have if you don't
care for each other.'

She spoke quietly, without rancour. 'Then why me,
Brad? Are you a little bored? Looking for adventure? A
new conquest?'

I stared at her. 'You're not being fair,' I answered. 'I
said before – I don't know. I don't know what it is between a man and woman that sets them on fire. I never

bothered much with women. I've been too busy.

'I know that I want you, that you have something for me and I for you that neither of us have ever known for anyone else. Don't ask me how I know it because I can't answer that either. I don't say that I can't live without you because I can. I can do without anything I must do without. I know that much.

'Life is made of many disappointments. but the individual survives them no matter how great they are. All I know right now is that I wouldn't like to do without you if I don't have to.'

There was a faint smile on her mouth. 'You're honest, Brad. Other men have offered more.'

'Honesty is the only luxury left in our society, and the most expensive.'

She took out another cigarette from her flat golden case and lit it. 'You better take me home now, Brad,' she said with a flame flecking dancing gold in her eyes.

Silently I turned on the ignition. The big motor hummed quietly as I backed the car out of the parking lot and headed back to town. We didn't exchange a word on the way back.

I stopped in front of her hotel and looked at her. 'Will I see you again, Elaine?'

She stared at me for a moment. 'I don't know, Brad. I don't know if we should.'

'Are you afraid of me?' I asked.

She shook her head. 'You're a strange man, Brad. No, I'm not afraid of you.'

'Are you afraid you'll fall in love with me?' I asked.

'No, I'm not afraid to fall in love with you,' she answered bluntly. 'I have nothing to be afraid of.' She opened the door and stepped out of the car. She stood looking in at me. 'But you, Brad; you'd better do some thinking. You're not free and you may be looking for trouble.'

'That's my headache,' I said quickly. 'Will I see you again?'

'Do what I say, Brad,' she said gently. 'Better think it over.'

'And when I do, if I still want to see you?' I persisted.

She shrugged her shoulders slightly. 'I still don't know. We'll see then.' She turned away. 'Good night, Brad.'

'Good night, Elaine.' I watched her walk into the hotel and disappear into the lobby before I put the car in gear.

Chapter SEVEN

It was almost eleven o'clock by the time I closed the garage doors and went up the walk to the house. I could see the lights in our bedroom from the walk and a curious discomfort came over me. For the first time I wished that Marge was not waiting up for me.

In a way I guess it was my own guilt feeling shaping up. At eleven o'clock Marge wouldn't be waiting up for me, it was just that it was too early for her to go to sleep. I paused in front of the door and lit a cigarette.

NEVER LEAVE ME

It was time I squared away with myself and levelled. Elaine had been right. I was overdue for a piece of thinking. What did I want with her anyway? If I was content, there was no need for me to look for trouble. Dames are dames.

I sat down on the porch steps and looked out into the night. Count your blessings, Brad, I told myself. You've got thirty grand worth of home, a hundred grand worth of business, two wonderful kids and a sweet, kind wife who knows you and understands you and you're used to. You have everything you wanted all the hungry years of your life; why try to change things now? Why become something you're not?

But there was something else nagging at me. Elaine. Her face. It was a picture out of a dream I once had. All the beauty I ever looked for in a woman, all the beauty I never thought was real.

I could hear her voice echoing in my mind, soft and low and warm. She was lonely, the way I had been when I was young and the world was a terrible place in which to be alone. She was afraid, the way I had been once. Afraid of the things life can do to you, with the fear that can only come from knowledge of what it has done.

I knew she liked me. I could tell that right away. People either went for me quick – or they didn't at all. Elaine went for me. I knew that the first day in the office when I had kept her from leaving. I was sure of it when she'd acted the way she did in the office today. And the clincher came when I kissed her.

Not the first time. The second. She kissed me then. And she wanted me, the way I wanted her. There was a hunger in her mouth that threatened to drain all my strength, a passion I had thought lost a long time ago had come up in me. I had been surprised at its intensity, and a little

60

frightened, too. That was why I had stopped. It made me realise suddenly that I was no different from any other man I knew. I didn't know whether I liked that or not.

'Hello, you.' Marge's voice came softly from behind me. 'What're you doing?'

I felt her hand press reassuringly down on my shoulder. Without turning around, I reached up and touched her hand. 'Thinking,' I said.

I heard a rustle of her clothing. 'Got a problem, Brad?' she asked sympathetically, sitting down on the step next to me. 'Tell Mamma. Maybe she can help.'

I looked at her. Her hair framed her face in a gentle oval, her mouth curved sweetly. That was something I liked about her. She could listen, she was willing to listen. But this was nothing I could tell her. This was something I would have to work out myself.

'No problem, baby,' I said slowly. 'I was just sitting here, thinking how good it is to get out of the city.'

Her eyes crinkled into a smile. She got to her feet, pulling me after her. 'In that case, nature boy,' she laughed, 'don't forget summer is over and you can catch cold sitting like this. Better come inside and while I fix coffee, you can tell me all about your dinner with Paul and Edith.'

I followed her through the living-room. 'Mrs Schuyler was with us too,' I said. 'I drove them out to the airport and then took her back to the hotel.'

She cast a mischievous look at me. 'Look out for these Washington widows, my boy,' she teased. 'They eat young men like you.'

'I feel sorry for her,' I said defending myself against nothing.

She was still in a teasing mood. 'Don't feel too sorry.' She turned the switch on under the coffee. 'Don't forget you have a wife and two children to take care of.'

'I won't forget,' I said seriously.

Something in my voice made her look up at me and the laughter faded from her eyes. She came over to me and looked up into my face. 'I know you won't, Brad,' she said quietly. Her lips brushed my cheek quickly. 'That's why I love you.'

The bright morning sun flooding into the bedroom woke me up. I stared vaguely at the ceiling. The room seemed somehow wrong to me, as if it were subtly out of place. Then I knew what it was. I was in Marge's bed.

I turned my head slowly. Her face was on the pillow next to me, her eyes open, looking into mine. She smiled.

I smiled back at her.

She whispered something.

I didn't hear her. 'What?' I asked, my voice shattering the morning quiet in the room.

'Young lover,' she whispered. 'I'd almost forgotten.'

I began to remember the night.

She put her arm up around my neck and drew my head down. 'You're a wonderful man, Brad,' she breathed into my ear. 'Do you know that?'

A pain began to choke my throat. I couldn't speak. How many men have made love to their wives because of the fires started by another woman? And which betrayal is more wrong? The real or the imaginary? Her hand was stroking my hair, her voice was still whispering in my ear.

I climbed into the car next to Jeanie. Marge looked down at us from the open doorway. 'Try to get home early, Brad,' she called. 'Dad's coming up for dinner tonight.'

'I'll be early,' I promised. Dad came up every Tuesday night.

Jeanie put the car into gear and we rolled down the driveway. We just skimmed the corner post and shot out into the street. I let out a sigh. 'Someday you're gonna hit that,' I said.

She looked over at me and grinned. 'Take it easy, Dad.'

'You take it easy,' I said.

She jammed on the brakes and stopped short for a traffic light. She turned towards me. 'Have you thought about what I said?'

'About what?' I asked, deliberately playing dumb.

'About an anniversary present for Mamma,' she said patiently.

'Oh, sure,' I said casually.

She was immediately excited. 'You did, Dad? Really? What are you getting her?'

'The light changed,' I said deliberately ignoring her questions.

'Bother the light, Dad,' she said, starting the car. 'What did you get her?'

'You'll see,' I said. 'When she gets it. It's a surprise and I'm not going to have you blab it out.'

'I'll keep the secret, Dad. Honest.' Her voice had lowered to a conspiratorial whisper.

'Promise?'

'I promise.'

'A mink coat.'

'Golly! Dad, that's terrif!'

'Take your foot off the accelerator or neither of us will be here to give it to her,' I said quickly.

She slammed on the brakes again. We were at her school. She opened the door, then she changed her mind and leaned across the seat and kissed my cheek. 'Dad, you're the greatest!'

I watched her running across the street and then slid

over under the wheel. Something bright on the floor of
the car caught my eye. I bent over and picked it up.

It shone brightly in the sunlight. It was a thin gold
cigarette case. I turned it over slowly in my hands. There
was a small block monogram up in the corner. One word

Elaine.

Chapter EIGHT

Matt Brady was a little man and I never saw him smile. His eyes were wide blue and unwinking. They looked right at you and through you. I didn't like him. I don't know why, but the minute I saw him I knew I wouldn't like him.

Maybe it was the suggestion of power that draped around his shoulders like an invisible cloak. Maybe it was the way all the other members of the committee acted towards him. Each was a big man in the business. Each headed a company that was worth many millions of dollars. Yet they bowed and scraped before him and called him Mister as if he were God. And he treated them as if they were his lowliest slaves.

I glanced quickly at Chris to see how I was doing. His face was impassive. I cursed him silently for being right so righteously and turned back to Matt Brady.

His voice was as cold as the rest of them. 'Young man,' he said, 'I don't have time to waste in idle conversation. I'm a blunt man and I come right to the point. Nowhere in your exposition have I been assured that we can reach the people with the type of campaign you are suggesting. That they would even understand what we're trying to say.'

I stared back at him steadily. I was damned if I could see how Elaine could call him sweet. 'Mr Brady,' I answered, 'I'm a public relations counsellor. You know what that is? A fancy name for the guy who comes to town ahead of the circus and puts up signs. Only I don't tell them to go to the circus. I tell them how much fun there is in living because of the circus.'

You couldn't sidetrack the old buzzard. Words meant nothing to him. His mind worked like a machine. I was beginning to understand how he'd got where he did. 'I don't doubt your abilities, young man,' he said. 'I just question your campaign. It seems sketchy and poorly thought out to me, as if your main concern is getting the account for yourself rather than perform a service for your client.'

You can go far with faking, then you got to throw the whole hog. 'Mr Brady,' I smiled gently. 'If I may have the same plivilege of bluntness that you claim for yourself I would like to say that you haven't the faintest idea of what I've been talking about. Because you are thinking selfishly of how this campaign would personally benefit Matt Brady's interests rather than the industry.'

I felt rather than heard the vague shock that stirred around the table. Chris stared disapprovingly at me.

Matt Brady's voice was deceptively smooth. 'Go on, young man.'

I stared into his eyes. Maybe I was crazy but I thought there was a twinkle of smile lurking in their depths. 'Mr Brady,' I said quietly. 'You make steel and I make opinions. I assume you know your business and when I buy anything made of your product – a car or a re-frigerator – I rely on the fact that you have supplied the proper kind of metal in it to do the job. The fact that you do keeps me buying.'

I turned from him and looked down the long table at his confreres. 'Gentlemen,' I continued, 'on the books of each of your companies you carry an item called good will. Some of you carry that item at a dollar, some of you carry it at a million dollars or more. I don't know the accounting method used to determine the value of that intangible. I'm not a book-keeper. I sell intangibles. You can't hold what I give you in your hands, you can't put it on a scale and weigh it, you can't count it and put it into inventory.'

They were interested now. I could tell from the looks on their faces. 'I deal in that item you call good will. If I may be permitted to recall for a moment some things people were saying about your business just a little while ago, I would like to remind you of them. They are not pleasant reminders, but, unfortunately, necessary to my argument.

'After the attack on Pearl Harbour, there was a com-mon saying here in New York that the Japanese had returned the Ninth Avenue El to us. And rightly or wrongly, they blamed you, the steel industry, for selling it to them. It didn't matter that the truth was greatly different from the rumour; what did matter was that for a long time you were resented for it.

'It didn't bother you then. You were not concerned with selling your product to the public, you were engaged in an all-out war effort. But it would have mattered if you had been dependent on the consumer for your livelihood at that time. I know. For in Ninteen Forty-two I was called down to Washington to help get the scrap metals drive out of its doldrums. And one of the main reasons it had not been doing as well as it should was because the people did not trust what you would do with that metal. We set up an educational campaign that the public accepted. Result: with the public's faith in you restored and the use for the metal clearly set forth – the flow of scrap to your rolling mills was most successful.'

I paused to catch my breath and take a sip of water from the tumbler in front of me. From the corner of my eye I could see that even Matt Brady had been interested in what I had said.

'Good will, gentlemen,' I began again. 'That's my business. I try to help people think kindly of you. I probably won't sell a ten-cent can opener for you.

'But if I'm successful people will think more highly of you than they do today. And the chances are that if they like you more, the many things you sell will be sold more easily. Whether you gentlemen realise it or not, it is just as important for you to have your customers like you as it is for the man in the candy store on your corner.

'And like it or not, gentlemen, as far as I'm concerned you're nothing but the guys in business in the biggest candy store on the biggest corner in the world.' I picked up the papers in front of me and began stuffing them into my briefcase. As far as I was concerned the meeting was over.

I didn't have to look down the table at Chris to confirm what I already felt. This was half a million bucks that would never show on our books ...

Chris hadn't said a word all the way down in the elevator. The air in the street seemed suddenly chill in spite of the bright sunshine. I pushed my collar up against my neck.

A cab pulled up to the kerb at his gesture. I was about to step into it when I changed my mind. I turned and gave him my briefcase. 'Go back to the office, Chris,' I said. 'I'm gonna walk around a bit.'

He nodded, taking the briefcase from me, and stepped into the cab. I watched it pull away from the kerb and stepped back into the crowds on Fifth Avenue. I put my head down, my hands in my coat pockets and started to walk uptown.

I was the biggest dope of all. I should have known better. But I still might've had it if not for Matt Brady, with his cold eyes and sceptical mouth. 'Beware of little men,' my father had once said. A little man had to be smarter to survive. Dad was right. Matt Brady was a little man. And smart. He saw right through to the phony that I was. A hatred for him began to build up in me. He knew everything, he had all the answers. At least that's what he thought. But he was wrong. Nobody had all the answers.

I don't know how long I'd been walking or where, but when I stopped, I was standing in front of her hotel. I looked up at it. The gold cigarette case in my pocket since the morning was cold against my fingers.

She was waiting at the door as I came down the hall from

the elevator. As soon as I saw her face I knew she had been expecting me.

I followed her into the room, the cigarette case in my hand. 'You left it in the car on purpose,' I said.

She took it from my hand silently, neither confirming nor denying. She didn't meet my eyes. 'Thanks, Brad,' she said.

'Why?'

Slowly she looked up at me. Again I could feel the strange loneliness in them. Her lips parted as if to speak but then her eyes filled with tears.

I held out my arms to her and she came into them as if she belonged there. Her face was against my chest and her tears were salty against my mouth.

I held her for a long time like that and at last the tears stopped. Her voice was very low. 'I'm sorry, Brad; I'll be okay now.'

I watched her cross the room. She disappeared into the bedroom and a few seconds later I could hear the sounds of running water. I threw my coat across a chair and picked up the phone.

Room service in this hotel was good. I just finished pouring some Scotch into the glasses when she came back.

Her face was scrubbed and clean and her eyes held no trace of the tears that had reddened them. I held a glass to her. 'You need a drink.'

'I'm sorry, Brad,' she apologised again. 'I didn't mean to cry.'

'Forget it,' I said quickly.

She shook her head vehemently. 'I hate crying,' she insisted. 'It's not fair to you.'

I sank into the chair beside my coat. 'All's fair in love

and – ' I started, but the expression on her face stopped me.

Silently I sipped at my drink. My nerves stopped jumping as the whisky hit my stomach and ricochetted through my system. She sat in a chair opposite me.

How long we sat there I'll never know. We didn't speak until I had refilled my glass and peace and contentment began to steal into me. The world and business were far away now, even the disappointment of a little while ago was gone.

Dusk had begun to shade the windows behind her, my voice echoed in the room. I had held up my glass and looked into it. The words had come from my lips and I hadn't expected them.

'I love you, Elaine.'

I lowered the glass and looked at her.

She was nodding her head. 'And I love you,' she answered.

Then I knew why she had nodded. It was as if we had both known all the time. I didn't move from the chair. 'I don't know how it happened, or why.'

'It doesn't matter,' she interrupted. 'But from the moment I saw you, I began to live again. I was alone.'

'You're not alone any more,' I said.

'No?' she questioned softly.

We came together in the centre of the room; there was a fire inside me.

I could feel the muscles of my body straining with an almost forgotten beat. My arms had a strength all their own and held her close to me.

Her arms tightened round my neck. I turned my face to her.

Her eyes stared at me, vague, unseeing; only her lips were moving. 'No, Brad, no. Please.'

I rose quickly to my feet and picked her up in my arms.

My voice was husky as I looked down at her. 'There is no word for it. This never happened before.' I pressed my lips to her mouth. 'Only to us.'

Her lips were warm and trembling, and slowly the trembling stopped and nothing but the warmth remained. She was a figurine in old ivory and the orange flush of the fading sun turned her flesh into a delicate gold.

Her body was like a fire that had been too long without a spark to make it flame and in a moment we were in a world all our own, on a cloud just across the moon, racing faster than light like an interplanetary rocket.

I found her mouth with my lips, and a comet caught me in its grip, then burst inside me like a shooting star. There was a startling moment of stillness and then I was tumbling into a bottomless void, a crazy thought trailing through my mind.

What a way to get even with Matt Brady for costing me half a million bucks!

Chapter NINE

The sound of running water woke me up. I lay there quietly, letting my eyes get used to the strange darkness. Instinctively I reached for my cigarettes. They were not in their usual place. It wasn't until that moment that I realised where I was.

I rolled over to the edge of the bed and sat up. I turned on the lamp on the night table and looked at my watch. Nine o'clock. Marge would be worried. I picked up the phone and gave the operator the number.

I could hear the dial clicking as the bathroom door opened and Elaine came out. She stood there a moment looking down at me, framed by the light in the doorway behind her. There was a small towel around her head and a large turkish towel wrapped around her body.

'Calling home?' It was more a statement than a question.

I nodded.

She didn't answer. Just then Marge's voice came on the phone. 'Brad?'

'Yeah,' I answered. 'Everything okay, baby?'

'Yes, Brad. Where are you? I was worried.'

'I'm okay,' I said into the phone, looking up at Elaine, still in the doorway. 'I been out drinking.'

'You sure you're all right?' she insisted. 'You sound funny.'

'I said I'm all right,' I replied impatiently. 'I just had a few drinks.'

Elaine went back into the bathroom and closed the door behind her. I picked up a cigarette and tried to light it.

'Where are you?' Marge asked. 'The office has been trying to locate you all afternoon.'

'I'm in a bar on Third Avenue,' I lied. 'What do they want?'

'I don't know,' she answered. 'Chris said it had something to do with the Steel Institute. He said for you to call him at home.' She hesitated a moment. 'What happened, Brad? It didn't go so good, did it?'

'No, it didn't,' I answered brusquely.

I could almost see her smile encouragingly through the phone. 'Don't feel bad about it, Brad. It's not that important. We can get along without it.'

'Yeah,' I said.

'Chris said you might have to run down to Pittsburgh to their main office. He didn't know, when I spoke to him last, but I packed your bag and sent it down to your office in case you need it. Are you going to call him now?'

'Yeah,' I answered.

Her voice brightened. 'You'll call me back and let me know what's happening, won't you?'

'Of course, baby,' I replied.

'I hope you didn't drink too much,' she said. 'You know how sick it makes you.'

'I didn't,' I answered. Suddenly I wanted to get off the phone. 'I'll call Chris now and call you right back.'

I put the phone down while her good-bye was still ringing in my ears. As if it were a signal, the bathroom door opened again and Elaine came out.

'You didn't have to do that,' I said. 'It wasn't private.'

Her eyes were very wide and thoughtful. 'I couldn't stand here and watch you lie.'

I tried to make a joke of it. 'No guts, eh?'

A shadow crossed her face. 'No guts,' she answered seriously. 'I told you that before.'

I reached towards her but she stepped around my outstretched hand. 'You have another call to make, haven't you?' she said pointedly.

'It can keep,' I said, catching up to her. I kissed her mouth, her body was warm through the towel.

Her arms were around my neck. 'Brad. Darling Brad.'

I kissed the hollow on her throat where there were still beads of water from the shower. 'I love you, Elaine,' I whispered. 'Like I never loved before, like I never thought I'd feel.'

I could hear her contented sigh as she snuggled closely against me. 'Tell me, Brad, tell me. Make me feel that

75

you're not lying, not playing with me. Tell me that you love me like I love you. Tell me.'

Chris's voice was excited when I finally called him. 'Where the hell have you been?'

'Drinking,' I answered succinctly. 'What's up?'

'I've been trying to reach you all afternoon,' he said. 'Brady wants to see you at his office in Pittsburgh tomorrow morning.'

His excitement began to run through me. The old pitch had crossed the plate after all. I was a fool to try to outguess the umpire. 'I'll get right out and get plane tickets,' I said.

'I got 'em already,' he replied quickly. 'They're out at the airport in your name. Flight one-oh-four, leaving at eleven-fifteen. And your valise is out there too, in the checkroom.'

I looked at my watch. It was almost ten o'clock, I would have to hurry. 'Okay, Chris. I'll get going.'

A note of relief came into his voice. 'Bring home the bacon, boss. Get that job and we'll all eat high off the hog.'

'Hog meat is for peasants,' I grinned. 'Trot out the fatted calf.'

I put down the phone and turned to Elaine. 'You heard?' I asked.

She nodded. 'Better hurry,' she said. 'There isn't much time.'

'You better hurry,' I smiled at her, 'and throw some things in a bag. You're coming with me.'

She sat up, startled. 'Brad, don't be a fool. You can't do that.'

I was already gathering my things together. 'Doll,' I said joking, 'you don't know me. I can do anything.

76

You're my good luck piece, and you're not getting out of my sight until this deal is signed, sealed and delivered.'

I called home while Elaine was packing her valise. 'I'm grabbing the eleven-fifteen plane to Pittsburgh,' I said.

'I was wondering why you didn't call right back,' Marge replied.

'I couldn't,' I said hurriedly. 'Chris's line was busy and I just caught him. Brady wants to see me.'

'Wonderful,' she laughed into the phone. 'I'm so proud of you, Brad. I just know you'll do good.'

Chris had taken care of everything. There was a note attached to my bag informing me that I had a suite reserved in my name at the Brooke in Pittsburgh. I signed the register and we went up to our room at about two in the morning.

She stood in the centre of the living-room while the bell-hop checked the suite. At last he came back to me, the key in his hand. I gave him a dollar and the door closed behind him.

I turned to her and smiled. 'Be it ever so humble, there's no place like home.'

She didn't answer.

'Don't be so grim, doll,' I said. 'Pittsburgh can't be that bad.'

At last she answered. 'I must have been crazy to let you do it. What if you run into someone you know?'

'What if you do?' I countered.

'I don't have to explain anything to anybody,' she replied. 'But you –'

I didn't let her finish. 'I'll do the worrying for me.'

'Brad,' she protested, 'you don't know what people will say, how they are, what they do –'

'And I don't care,' I interrupted her again. 'I don't give a damn about people. All I care about is you. I want you near me, close to me. I don't want to be away from you now that I've found you. I've spent too long a time waiting for you.'

She came very close to me, her eyes searching my face. 'Brad, you mean that, don't you?'

I nodded. 'We're here, ain't we? That's answer enough.'

Her eyes were still on my face. I don't know what she sought there, but she must have seen what she wanted. My voice stopped her before she got to the door. She turned to face me.

'Wait a minute, Elaine,' I said. 'We gotta do things right.' I scooped her up in my arms and carried her across the threshold.

Chapter TEN

The administration building of Consolidated Steel was new and shining-white, just inside the steel wire grating that fenced their property. Behind the building lay the black, soot-covered foundries, their chimneys belching flame and smoke into the clear blue sky.

A uniformed special officer stopped me as I came through the door. 'Mr Rowan to see Mr Brady,' I said.

'Do you have a pass?' he asked.

I shook my head.

'An appointment?'

'Yes.'

He picked up a telephone on a table near him and whispered into it, all the while watching me carefully. I lit a cigarette while waiting for him to pass me. I had time to take just one pull when he put the phone down. 'This elevator, Mr Rowan,' he said politely and pressed a button on the wall.

The elevator door opened and there was a second uniformed special officer in the elevator. 'Mr Rowan to Mr Brady's office,' said the first officer as I went into the elevator.

The doors closed behind me and the elevator began its ascent. I looked at the operator. 'This is almost as bad as getting to see the President,' I smiled.

'Mr Brady is Chairman of the Board,' the special officer dead-panned.

For a moment I fought an impulse to tell him that I was talking about the President of the United States but it would have been wasted so I kept my mouth shut. The elevator stopped and the doors opened. I stepped out.

The special officer was right behind me. 'This way, sir.'

I followed him down a deserted marble corridor, past a series of pine-panelled doors. Between each door was an electric light in the form of a torch in the hand of a classic Greek figure. At almost any moment I expected one of the doors to open and an undertaker to come out to direct us to the remains.

He paused in front of one of the doors, knocked lightly, then opened it and waved me in. I blinked my eyes at the light in the room after the gloomy corridor and heard the door close behind me.

'Mr Rowan?' The girl at the large semicircular desk in the centre of the room looked up at me inquiringly.

I nodded and walked towards her.

She got up and came around her desk. 'Mr Brady is tied up at the moment and extends his apologies. Would you care to wait in the reception room, please?'

I let out a silent whistle. After this, nobody could tell me that the only thing Matt Brady had on his mind was steel. Not with a babe like this for a secretary. This kid was built for long-distance hauling and she had the equipment that went with endurance.

'Must I?' I smiled.

The smile was wasted, for she turned and led me to another door. I followed her slowly, enjoying the clockwork. This was a dame who knew what she had and made no bones about it. As a matter of fact I couldn't see a bone anywhere. She held the door open for me.

I stopped and looked at her. 'How come you ain't wearing one of them special cop uniforms?' I asked her.

She didn't smile. 'Make yourself comfortable,' she said formally. 'If there's anything you'd like, please call me.'

'Is that legit?' I grinned.

For the first time an expression appeared on her face. She looked puzzled.

I laughed aloud. 'D'you mean that?' I translated.

The puzzled frown vanished. 'Of course,' she replied. 'Cigars and cigarettes are in the humidor on the table. Magazines and papers on the rack beside it.' She closed the door before I had chance to say anything else.

I looked around the room. It was richly and quietly furnished. The walls were oak-panelled, the heavy furniture of comfortable leather. The carpets were thick and seemed to come up to your ankles. My eye was caught by a group of photographs neatly framed, hung in a cluster on the wall opposite the door.

I walked over to them. Some very familiar faces looked

down at me. Seven photographs all autographed to Matt Brady personally. All Presidents of the United States. Woodrow Wilson, Harding, Coolidge, Hoover, F.D.R., Truman and Eisenhower.

I ground out my cigarette in a tray. No wonder the operator hadn't gone for my joke. Presidents come and go but Matt Brady went on forever. I sat down and stared up at the photographs. Tough little man, Matt Brady. Smart. He didn't keep these pictures in his office like any other man would, where he could point to them or ignore them consciously to impress his visitors. He kept them in his waiting room as if to keep them in their place.

I began to wonder what I was doing here. Any guy who had as highly developed a sense of public psychology as Matt Brady seemed to have didn't need a guy like me for anything. I looked at my watch. I had already been in the room about five minutes. If I had it figured right, it would be ten minutes before he would call for me. By then I would have had time to absorb the psychological effect of the waiting room.

I grinned to myself. For a moment he almost had me. But two can play at that game. I got out of the chair and opened the door.

The girl looked up at me, a startled expression in her eyes. I picked a magazine from the rack. 'Where's the washroom?' I asked.

Silently she pointed to a door opposite me. I crossed the office quickly. As I opened the washroom door her voice caught me. 'Mr Brady will be free in a few minutes.'

'Ask him to wait,' I said, quickly closing the door behind me.

I had been in the can almost ten minutes when the door opened and someone came in. From under the tile booth door I could see a pair of men's shoes stand hesitantly in front of the booth. They were cops' shoes. I didn't have to see the grey trouser cuffs to know that. I grinned and kept silent. A few seconds later the shoes went away and the door slammed again.

It had taken a long time, but one of my father's predictions had just come true. Years ago I remembered him saying to my mother that the only way they would ever get me out of the bathroom was to get the cops after me.

I sat there and flipped the pages of the magazine. About five minutes later the door slammed again. I looked down under the booth. A pair of small shiny black shoes went past. I smiled grimly to myself. This round was mine.

Quickly I dropped the magazine to the floor. A second later I came out of the booth, and crossed over to the washstand.

The little man standing there looked up at me questioningly. I grinned down at him in apparent surprise. 'Mr Brady,' I said, 'what nice offices you have here!'

Matt Brady's own office was big enough to serve as the lobby for Radio City Music Hall. It was on a corner of the building and two of its walls were large picture windows through which one could see building after building, all bearing the gleaming stainless steel signs reading Consolidated Steel. His desk occupied the large corner where the two windows came together. Around his desk were three bucket chairs facing him. On the opposite side of the office was a long conference table with ten chairs and a long sectional couch took up the closed corners of the room. In front of the couch was a marble-topped coffee table and two more chairs.

He motioned me to a seat and went behind his desk. He sat down silently and looked at me. I waited for him to speak. His first question came from left field. 'How old are you, Mr Rowan?'

I looked at him curiously. 'Forty-three,' I answered.

His next question also caught me off base. 'How much do you earn a year?'

'Thirty-five thousand,' I said quickly, before I had a chance to lie.

He nodded silently and looked down at his desk. There were some typewritten sheets on it. He seemed to be studying them. I waited for him to continue to speak. After a moment he looked up at me. 'Do you know why I sent for you?' he asked.

'I thought I did,' I said honestly. 'But now I'm not quite sure.'

He smiled mirthlessly. 'I believe in honest talk, young man,' he said. 'So I won't waste time in coming to the point. How would you like to make sixty thousand a year?'

I laughed nervously. The way this guy threw numbers around, I was beginning to feel as if I was back in Washington. 'I'd like it,' I said.

He leaned towards me confidentially. 'At yesterday's meeting you presented a plan for the benefit of the industry. Remember?'

I nodded, not trusting myself to speak. I also remembered that he didn't think very much of it.

'There were certain flaws in your presentation,' he continued. 'But basically, it was sound.'

I let my breath escape through my lips gently. The big one hadn't got off the hook after all. A glow of triumph began to fill me. 'I'm glad you think so, sir,' I said quickly.

'When I left the meeting, I must admit I was slightly angry,' he said, still in a confidential tone of voice. His eyes held mine. 'Because of your accusation.'

'I regret it, sir,' I said quickly. 'It was only because –'

He held up a magnanimous hand, interrupting me. 'Say no more. I admit I gave you sufficient provocation. But what you said impressed me. You were the only one there who had the nerve to call a spade a spade.' He smiled wryly. 'It's been too long a time since anyone spoke to me like that.'

By now I was going around in circles. I didn't know what the devil he wanted, so I kept quiet. They never hanged a man for keeping his mouth shut.

He waved his hand at the windows behind him. 'See that, Mr Rowan?' he said. 'That's Consolidated Steel, and that's not all of it, either. There are twenty other foundries like it in the United States. It's one of the five largest corporations in the world – and I made it what it is today. Many people didn't approve of my methods, but that didn't matter. What did matter was that I made a dream come true. I've eaten, slept and drunk steel since I was a twelve-year-old water carrier in a foundry.'

In spite of myself I was impressed by the little man. His tone had all the fervour of an evangelist. I kept silent.

'So when you said that I was thinking selfishly you were absolutely right. I make no apologies for it. Too many years have gone by, and I'm too old to change now.'

I still couldn't see what he was driving at, so I waited. He leaned back in his chair and looked at me. I took a cigarette and lit it. He let me take a pull before he spoke. It was a good thing he did because what he said almost knocked me off my seat.

'I like you, Mr Rowan,' he said quietly. 'Because you're like me. You're all the things you would say I was. Tough. Selfish. Ruthless. But I would call it practical. A recognition of the laws of survival.

'That's why I asked you to come and see me. I'm prepared to offer you a job here as Vice-President and Director of Public Relations at sixty thousand dollars a year. I need a man with your talents for organisation to do for Consolidated Steel what you plan to do for the industry.'

I held on to my chair. 'But what of the industry campaign?' I asked.

He laughed shortly. 'Let them worry about their own campaign,' he said succinctly.

I was silent. This was hitting it. All my life I had been waiting for a kick like this. Now that it had come I couldn't believe it.

Matt Brady spoke again. Apparently he had taken my stunned silence for an assent. The mirthless smile was back on his face. His fingers tapped the typewritten sheets of paper on his desk. 'Mr Rowan, these papers are as complete a dossier of your life as I could gather overnight. As you see I like to know as much as possible about my associates and I feel I only have to talk on one small point.'

I looked at him questioningly. My head was still reeling. What was he talking about now?

He looked down at the papers and spoke. 'Your business record is a very good one, there is nothing there I have need to speak to you about. Your home life is also good. But there are portions of your personal life I think you must be cautioned about.'

A chill began to settle down on me. 'What, Mr Brady?'

'Last night you checked into the Brooke with a woman who is not your wife, Mr Rowan. That's very indiscreet. We at Consolidated must remember we are constantly under surveillance.'

I began to get angry. How long had this guy been

watching me? Maybe this was his payoff to get me away from Elaine. 'By whom, Mr Brady?' I asked coldly. 'Who could be interested enough in me to know what I've been doing?'

'Everyone who has anything to do with steel in Pittsburgh must expect to be watched, Mr Rowan,' he said.

I had to find out what was on those sheets of paper. 'I suppose your spies also gave you the name of the lady with me last night?' I asked.

He looked up at me coldly. 'I'm not interested in the names of your sleeping companions, Mr Rowan. I'm only mentioning this because of our planned association.'

I got out of my chair. 'I've decided I'm not interested in your offer, Mr Brady.'

He got to his feet. 'Don't be foolish, young man,' he said quickly. 'No woman is worth it.'

I laughed shortly. I wondered what he would say if he knew it was his niece we were talking about. 'That hasn't anything to do with it, Mr Brady,' I said coldly. I walked to the door and opened it.

A special officer sitting just outside the door scrambled to his feet. He looked at me expectantly.

I looked back into the office at the little man standing behind his desk. 'You're overdoing this cop thing a bit, Mr Brady,' I said. 'Even the gestapo couldn't help Hitler when the chips were down.'

Chapter ELEVEN

I hit the street under a full head of steam. The bright sun tore at my eyes and I blinked. Down the street was Oscar's bar. Its cool, dark interior looked good to me. I pushed my way through the revolving door.

It was one of those cocktail lounges with restaurant attached. I headed for the bar and climbed up on the stool. The place was loaded with Con Steel people. I could tell from the badges on their clothing. This was a white-collar joint; the foundry workers apparently had their own stamping grounds.

The bartender slid over in front of me. 'Double Black Label over rocks,' I said. 'Lemon twist.'

He threw three ice cubes into a tumbler and put it down in front of me. Reaching behind him, he brought down a bottle of Black Label and filled the tumbler three-quarters full. Then he twisted a cut of lemon peel over the glass and dropped it in. 'Buck and a half,' he said.

Either the nut was nothing here or they cut the liquor big. I dropped a five on the bar and picked up my drink. 'Ride it,' I said. I needed time to think.

Those sheets of paper on Matt Brady's desk bothered me. Whoever made that report might know Elaine was with me. That wouldn't be good. Matt Brady might ignore my words, but I was sure he wouldn't forgive me having her with me. I'd give an eyetooth to know who sent him that report.

I thought about Elaine back at the hotel waiting for me. I remembered how she had been at breakfast that morning. I had been nervous. My stomach had been jumping.

'Easy, boy, easy,' she had said with quick understanding. 'Uncle Matt isn't an ogre. He won't eat you. He just wants to talk over a deal.'

In spite of myself I had smiled. Maybe it was just a deal to Matt Brady, but it was the big deal to me.

I took another sip of my drink and ran into water. Silently I gestured to the bartender for a refill. I sure kicked that one out the window. I looked down at my watch. Two o'clock. I hated to go back to the hotel and tell her what had happened.

I was on my second double when I looked up at the mirror over the bar. I thought a dame had smiled at me. I was right. The girl in the mirror smiled again.

I spun around on my chair and smiled back at her. She gestured and I picked up my drink and walked towards her table. It was Matt Brady's secretary. I felt a little tight. My mouth twisted in a bitter smile. 'How come the old man let you out for lunch?' I asked. 'The Department of Labour get after him?'

She ignored my crack. 'Mr Brady always leaves the office at one-thirty,' she said. 'He doesn't come back.'

I knew an invitation when I heard one. I dropped into the chair beside her. 'Good,' I said. 'I hate drinking alone.'

She smiled. 'He called your hotel and left a message for you before he went home.'

'Tell him to keep it,' I said belligerently. 'I want no part of him.'

She held up her hands as if to ward off a blow. 'Don't be mad at me, Mr Rowan,' she said. 'I only work there.'

She was right. I was being a fool. 'I'm sorry, Miss – uh – Miss – '

'Wallace,' she answered. 'Sandra Wallace.'

'Miss Wallace,' I said formally. 'Let me get you a drink.' I signalled the waiter and looked at her inquiringly.

'Very dry martini,' she said. The waiter went away and she looked at me. 'Mr Brady likes you,' she said.

'Good,' I answered. 'I don't like him.'

'He wants you to work for him. He was sure that you would. He even had the legal department draw up a contract for you.'

'Does he have an employment contract with spies too?' I asked.

The waiter put her drink down and went away. I picked up my drink and waved it at her. 'The only job I'd take from him right now is watching you,' I said.

She laughed. 'You're crazy.'

'Crazy as hell,' I said. 'For that he wouldn't even have to pay me.'

'Thank you, Mr Rowan,' she said, raising her glass to her lips.

'Brad's the name; whenever somebody calls me Mister, I always turn around. I think it's my father they're talking to.'

'Okay, Brad,' she smiled. 'But sooner or later you'll get used to it and do what he wants.'

'You heard me when I went out of the office,' I told her. 'I'm not taking his job.'

A strange look came over her face. It was almost as if she had heard this many times before. 'He'll get you, Brad,' she said quietly. 'You don't know him. Matt Brady always gets what he wants.'

A flash of understanding suddenly penetrated my fuzzy head. 'You don't like him?' I asked.

She lowered her voice almost to a whisper. 'I hate him.'

My head was clearing quickly. 'Then why stay? You don't have to work for him. There are other jobs.'

'From the time I was eleven years old and my father was killed in the foundry I knew I was going to be his secretary.'

I was interested. 'How come?'

'My mother went to his office and dragged me with her. I was big for my age, and Matt Brady didn't miss a trick. I remember him walking around that desk and taking my hand. I even remember how cold his fingers were when he spoke to my mother.

' "Don't worry, Mrs Wolenciwicz," he said. "I'll give you enough money to live on, and when Alexandra grows up she can come and work for me here. Maybe even be my secretary."

'He never forgot what he said. Every now and then he

would call my mother to check and find out if I was taking the right courses and how I was doing in school.' She picked up her martini and stared into it. 'If I left him now, he'd never let me get another job.'

'Even if you left town?' I asked.

Her smile was bitter. 'I tried that once. He very quietly loused me up, and then generously gave me my job back.'

I took a sip of my drink. It tasted crummy in my mouth. I put it back on the table. I was through drinking for the afternoon. I took a deep breath. 'He keeping you?' I asked bluntly.

She shook her head. 'No,' she answered. 'A lot of people around the place think so, but he never so much as said a word to me that didn't have to do with business.' Her eyes were full on my face. There was a puzzled look in them as if she were asking me to explain it to her. 'I don't get it,' she added.

I stared at her for a full minute before I spoke. 'Does he have you watched too?' I asked.

'I don't know,' she said. 'Sometimes I think he does, sometimes I think not. He doesn't trust anybody.'

I had the feeling I could trust this dame. 'Did you see the report he had on me?'

She shook her head. 'It comes from personnel investigation office. It's given to him personally in a sealed envelope.'

'Is there any way I can get a copy?' I asked.

'There's only one copy and it's in his desk.'

'Can you get a look at it?' I persisted. 'I have to see it. He may have something in there that may mean big trouble for me.'

'It won't do any good, Brad,' she said. 'If there is anything he would never forget it.'

'But I would have a chance if I knew what he knew,' I said quickly.

She didn't speak. I could see she was a little frightened over having told me as much as she did. After all, she didn't know me from Adam. For all she knew, I could be one of Matt Brady's spies.

'A favour for a favour,' I said quickly. 'You help me, I help you. Get me a look at that report and I'll get you away from Matt Brady – so that he'll never find you.'

She took a deep breath and suddenly I was conscious of what had caught my eye back in her office. She had a terrific pair of lungs and for a moment I thought she was going to bust out of her dress. She saw me goggling at her and a peculiar smile came to her lips.

'I'm not hiding it there,' she said pointedly.

'I wish you were,' I said, dragging my eyes back to her face. 'But I got no luck. That would make business a pleasure.'

A faint flush crept into her cheeks. 'What makes you think it can't be?' she asked huskily.

Chapter TWELVE

We walked in through the big steel gate and I turned towards the building entrance. Her hand touched my arm. 'This way,' she said.

I followed her around the corner of the building. There, hidden in an arch of private hedges, was a door. She took a key from her bag and opened it. 'Matt Brady's private entrance,' she exclaimed.

We were in a small corridor. A few feet from the door was an elevator. She pressed the button and its doors opened. We stepped inside and she turned to me smiling. 'Matt Brady's private elevator,' she said. I felt the elevator begin to climb. She was still smiling at me.

There was no refusing that invitation. I pulled her towards me. Her eyes were wide open as her arms went up around my neck and her lips opened under mine. I was right the first time. This kid was built for distance. She was still hanging on, even after the doors had opened.

At last she came up for air. Her eyes were shining. 'I like you,' she said.

I managed a grin. I had to play it safe.

'You're my kind of guy,' she said. 'I knew it from the minute you made him come and get you out of the washroom.'

I didn't say a word.

'Damn!' she said, her eyes still on mine.

That surprised me. 'Why?' I asked.

Instead of explaining, she turned and started from the elevator. I followed her into Matt Brady's private office. She walked around his desk and took a key from her purse. She hesitated a moment, then opened the desk and took out the report. 'I'm a fool,' she said, the paper still in her hand. 'You can turn copper on me.'

I didn't answer, just stood there watching her. A moment passed; then without looking at it, she handed the paper to me. For the second time in a few seconds she had surprised me. 'Aren't you even going to look at it?' I asked.

She walked around me to her door and opened it. She stood there in the open doorway, looking back at me. 'No,' she said. 'I know you're married, and it isn't that I mean. But if another girl's got you, I don't want to know her name.'

The door closed behind her and I walked over to the

window to get the light. I tipped my hat figuratively to Matt Brady. He may not have had much time in which to work, but there was very little that he had missed. My whole life was down there in those few sheets of paper. I scanned the sheets searchingly for her name.

I had nothing to worry about. The report merely stated that I had been accompanied by a woman who spent the night in my suite and that pursuant to instructions they would discontinue further observation. I dropped the papers on his desk and lit a cigarette.

I just had time enough for one drag when the door opened. 'Well?' she asked.

'I read it,' I answered, pointing to the sheets.

'Everything all right?' She came into the room, closing the door behind her.

'Yeah,' I answered, beginning to feel a little foolish. I moved towards her. 'I don't know how to thank you,' I added awkwardly.

She didn't answer.

I moved towards the elevator. 'I guess I'd better be going.'

'You can't go right now,' she said. 'You'd be noticed. They'll see the elevator signal on the control panel in the lobby and they'll come to check.'

I stopped. 'How do I get out of here then?'

A curious smile crossed her lips. 'You have to wait for me. I leave about five-fifteen, when the rush is over.'

I checked my watch. It was almost four o'clock. The smile was still on her lips as she watched me. 'Sit down and wait,' she said. 'I'll get you a drink.'

I crossed the room to the large sectional and sank on to it. 'I can use one,' I said.

I watched her move about the office as she put the drink together. The ice cubes made a comforting clinking sound as she brought the glass over to me. I sipped it gratefully.

She slipped into a chair opposite me. 'What are you going to do now, Brad?' she asked.

I took another pull at my drink. 'Go back to New York and forget all about this,' I answered.

'It won't be as easy as that,' she said. 'Matt Brady wants you.'

I smiled at her.

'Don't smile,' she said seriously. 'When you get back to the hotel, you'll find a message there, asking you to dinner at his house this evening.'

'I won't go,' I said.

'You'll go,' she answered. 'By the time you get back to your hotel, you'll have thought it over. You'll remember all the money he was talking about, you'll think about everything you can do with it and everything it can do for you.' She sipped her drink. 'You'll go.'

'You know all the answers,' I said, watching her.

Her eyes fell from mine. 'I don't,' she replied. 'But I've seen this happen before. He'll get you. Money means nothing to him. He'll pile it in front of you until your head spins. He'll talk soft and tell you how great you are and how important you'll be. And all the time you'll be watching the pile of chips on the table grow until your eyes pop. Then tag – you've had it.'

I put my drink on the coffee table in front of me. 'Why are you telling me this?' I asked. 'What's in it for you?'

She put her drink on the table next to mine. 'I've seen many big and important people crawl to Matt Brady. It made me sick to see such fear.' Her voice trailed away and her eyes watched my face.

'So?' I asked softly.

'You're big and strong and cocky. And there was no

smell of fear around you. You weren't so frightened that you couldn't see me, that you thought I was a piece of furniture. I saw the way you looked at me.'

'How'd I look at you?' I asked.

She got to her feet and stood very straight before me. Then, slowly, she walked around the coffee table, towards me. I looked up at her, my eyes following every motion of her. She stopped in front of me and looked down. 'Like you're looking at me now,' she said.

I was silent. I made no move towards her.

That strangely curious smile came back to her lips. 'I know you're not for me,' she said. 'I know another woman's got you. And you know it too. I knew it when you kissed me. But that makes no difference.

'To you I'm not Matt Brady's secretary, not a fixture in his office. I'm a human being, a separate identity, a woman. That's the way you look at me.'

I didn't say a word. The only thing of value on this earth was that each of us was an individual and not a cog in a machine. No man was better than another because of circumstance or fortune, but each important to his own.

I reached for my drink, but her hand caught mine and stopped it. I looked up at her, our eyes met and locked.

A pulse in my temple began to bang. I don't know what made me stop. The price was right. She had everything a guy could want in a dame – except one thing. Love was missing. I was not for her.

Reluctantly I pushed her away. I didn't want to hurt her. I didn't know what to say.

She stared into my face. 'There is another woman, isn't there?'

I nodded.

She took a deep breath and got to her feet. I looked up

at her. There was a tremulous smile on her lips as she spoke. 'That's another thing I can like about you. You're honest. You don't cheat for cheating's sake alone.'

She went back into her office, and in a few minutes I could hear the faint clacking of her typewriter. The minutes dragged away slowly. I walked over to the window and looked out at the foundries. Matt Brady had a right to be proud. If circumstances were different I could even learn to like the guy. But they weren't. Maybe it was because what he said was true. We were too much alike.

Somewhere in the corridor outside the office a chime rang. Its mellow tone was still hanging in the air when she came back into the office. I turned to face her.

'It's okay now. We can leave in a few minutes,' she said.

Chapter THIRTEEN

I picked up a taxi in front of the gate and was back at the hotel at a quarter to six. Strange thing, the male ego, and I suppose I have enough of it to do justice to six people. I felt good. Show me another guy who could turn down sixty grand and a luscious babe all in the same day.

I was proud of myself and I couldn't wait to tell Elaine what a great man I was. I flung open the door of the suite and called out. 'Elaine!'

There was no answer.

I closed the door behind me and saw a note propped up on the foyer table. My elation vanished like water down the drain and my heart sank in sudden apprehension. She couldn't have gone and left me. She couldn't!

I picked it up and relief ran through me like a breath of cool wind in a heat spell.

4.30 p.m.

'DARLING,

A woman can stand only so much. Then she goes to the beauty parlour. Should be back by six-thirty.

Love you,

ELAINE.'

I dropped the note on the table and crossed the room to the telephone. I picked it up and put in a call to the office.

Chris's voice was excited. 'How'd you make out, Brad?'

'Not so good,' I answered. 'Brady wanted me to dump the whole deal and come to work for him.'

'What did he offer?'

'Sixty grand a year,' I said. I could hear Chris whistle even without the phone. 'He likes me,' I added caustically.

A note of satisfaction came into Chris's voice. 'When do you start?' he asked.

'I don't,' I said flatly. 'I turned him down.'

'You're crazy!' he said incredulously. 'Nobody in his right mind turns down that kind of money.'

'Better reserve a room for me at the Cornell Clinic, then,' I said, 'because that's what I did.'

'But, Brad!' he protested. 'It's the kind of setup you've been looking for. You can take the job and keep your interest here on the quiet. I can handle this end for you and there'd be a nice melon for us to cut up each year.'

There was a note in his voice I had never heard before. An echo of ambition, a cold desire to be top dog. I didn't like the way we suddenly had become partners. 'I said I didn't want the job, Chris,' I said coldly. 'And I'm still boss. The only thing I'm looking for is the industry account.'

'If you cross Matt Brady,' he said, the ambition dying painfully in his voice, 'you can forget the account.'

'That's my headache,' I said flatly.

'Okay, Brad, if that's the way you want it,' he said.

'That's the way I want it,' I answered.

There was an awkward pause for a moment, then came the question. 'Coming back tonight?'

The answer sprang quickly to my lips. 'No. Tomorrow. I have another meeting with Brady tonight.'

'Shall I call Marge and tell her?' he asked formally.

'I'll call her,' I said. 'See you tomorrow.'

'Keep punching,' he said as we hung up, but there was no enthusiasm in his voice.

I gave the operator my home number. I had time to pour myself a drink before Marge came on the wire. It tasted good. I was beginning to like the stuff, I thought grimly, as I heard her voice.

'Hello, baby,' I said.

Her voice was pleased. 'Brad.' She knew me too well to ask what had happened. I would tell her soon enough. 'You sound tired.'

I'd only said two words and she knew I was beat. 'I'm okay,' I said quickly. 'That Brady's a rough deal.'

'Were you at his office all day?' she asked.

I was glad she put it that way. At least I wouldn't have to lie. 'Yeah,' I said. 'He offered me a job. Sixty grand a year.'

'You don't sound happy about it,' she said.

'I'm not,' I said. 'I turned it down. I don't like him.'

I had a fast moment of misery at the faith in her answer.

'You know what you're doing, Brad,' she said without hesitation.

'I hope so,' I said. 'It might mean missing out on the whole steel account.'

'There'll be others,' she said. 'I'm not worried.'

'I'll know more before the night's over,' I said quickly. 'I'm going over to his house for dinner.'

'Whatever you do is all right with me,' she said.

Her trust was making me uncomfortable. I got off the subject quickly. 'How's Jeanie?'

'She's fine,' Marge answered. 'But she's acting very mysterious. She keeps hinting to me about a surprise for our anniversary. I wonder what she has up her sleeve.'

'Nothing but her arm, if I know her,' I laughed. The odds were even money she would tell Marge about the coat before the anniversary arrived. 'Hear anything from Brad?'

'A letter came this morning. He still has his cold and is staying in bed a few days. I'm worried.'

'Don't worry, baby,' I said. 'He'll be okay.'

'But if he's in bed he must be sick. You know how he is.'

'He's probably no more sick than I am,' I said. 'He's just grabbing a few days off from school.'

'But –'

'Nothing's wrong, baby. Stop worrying. I'll see you tomorrow.'

'Okay, Brad,' she said. 'Hurry home. I miss you.'

'I miss you too, baby,' I said. 'Bye.'

I put down the phone, added more Scotch and ice to my drink and put my feet up on the couch. I felt strange.

There was something wrong with me, but I didn't dig it. Old man Conscience should be kicking my teeth in by now but he wasn't even giving me any attention. Maybe Matt Brady's girl was wrong; maybe I wasn't any different than all those other jokers. Could be I was a natural-born cheatin' man with only room for one dame at a time. Or maybe I got to it a little late. I don't know.

Elaine. Her name came into my mind and I smiled at the thought of her. If ever there was a woman made for man, she was it. Everything about her was class and sheer delight. Her eyes, her trim tight little figure and the way she walked. I took another pull on my drink and closed my eyes to see her better. It was like turning off the lights to dream, and I did.

In the dream she was the little girl who lived on Sutton Place. I remember I used to go over from our railroad flat on Third Avenue just under El tracks to watch her. She was so pretty with her long hair and her primly-dressed governess always hovering near her.

She never even looked at me until one day her blue and red ball rolled over to me. I picked it up and shyly held it towards her.

She took it silently, as if it were her due that I should fetch it for her, and turned away. But her governess made her turn around and thank me. Her voice was like a tinkling bell in the city streets.

'Merci,' she said.

I stared at her for one wonderful moment, then turned and ran all the way home and up three flights of stairs to ask my mother what it meant.

'I think it means "thank you" in French,' Mum said.

I felt a hand on my shoulder and woke up. Elaine was smiling down at me. 'Drunk again,' she said.

I grinned and pulled her down to me. I caught her face in my hands and kissed her. We went so good together. After a moment she pulled loose.

'Hey!' she exclaimed. 'What's that for?'

'For love,' I answered.

She smiled and kissed me again. The whole world disappeared and when I got back to earth I was warm with the radiance of her being.

'Merci,' I said.

Chapter FOURTEEN

I watched the lights of the airport rise to meet me. I felt the plane touch the ground, first lightly, as if testing its ability to hold us, then firmly, as lights enfolded us in its embrace.

'I still think it's silly,' I said, turning to Elaine.

She looked from the window to me. 'No more silly than your refusing to see Uncle Matt tonight,' she said. 'You might have been able to work something out with him.'

I was irritated. I had told her everything but one. I hadn't mentioned that he had a report on me since I checked into the hotel. I didn't want to upset her. 'I told you before,' I said coldly, 'I don't want to work for him. I like business for myself.'

The plane rolled to a stop and I unfastened the landing belt. I leaned over and helped her.

'I'm sure something could have been done,' she insisted stubbornly. 'I could have gone with you and helped. But you and your pride – not wanting to take advantage of my knowing you.'

I was even more angry because I couldn't tell her the real reason I didn't dare take her with me to see Brady. After that report, all he would need was one look at her and I'd be dead for sure. I didn't answer, just waited for her to get up.

'The least you could have done was call up and say you weren't coming,' she continued.

I blew a fuse. I said vehmently, 'I don't give a damn what he thinks.'

We came out on to the runway and I picked up our bags and silently headed for the cab stand. I stalked angrily along, my eyes watched the ground before me.

Suddenly she began to laugh. I turned and looked at her, puzzled. 'What're you laughing at?' I demanded.

'You,' she smiled broadly. 'You look like a little boy who's being crossed at every turn.'

I had to smile. She was right. Nothing had gone the way I wanted ever since I told her that her uncle wanted me over at his house for dinner and I wouldn't go. Then I wanted to spend the night there and she insisted that we go back to New York. We caught a nine o'clock plane and spent the whole flight arguing about whether I should have gone to see him or not.

'That's better,' she said. 'That's the first smile I've seen on your face all night. If you are going to the office in the morning, it's better that you be fresh than all beat up from a bumpy flight. We'll be much more comfortable in my place in the Towers.'

'Okay,' I grumbled, waving towards a cab.

The taxi rolled to a stop in front of us. I opened the door and pushed the bags in, then followed Elaine into the cab. 'The Towers, driver,' I said.

I had just settled back into my seat and was lighting a cigarette when the driver's voice floated back to me.

'A fine thing it is, Bernard, when you don't recognise your old man's hack.'

'Pop!' His face grinned back at me in the match's flickering light. The car went into gear and swooped around the curve towards the exit. 'For God's sake, Pop!' I wound up yelling. 'Look where you're going.'

The back of his head shook dolefully. 'A sad night, a sad night.' The echoes of laughter were deep in his throat. 'When you were a lad, you could recognise me car six blocks away, and now –'

'Can it, Pop,' I began to laugh. 'It was never your back I knew, just the crazy way you drive. Some day they're gonna get wise to you. Then – bang – no medallion.'

He stopped for a signal light and looked up into the mirror.

'I spoke to Marge this afternoon. She told me you were in Pittsburgh an' didn't know whether you'd be back tonight or tomorrow. A big deal, she said.'

I could see his glance flickering across Elaine. I half smiled to myself as the car started again. Pop was a true hackie. Always ready to think the worst of anyone. It amused me to find I wasn't exempt from his suspicions.

'It was a big one, Pop,' I said. 'But like in the old fish story, it got away.'

Pop wasn't to be sidetracked. 'And the lady? A business friend, no doubt?' he asked dryly.

I glanced at Elaine out of the corner of my eyes. She caught on quick. There was an amused smile on her lips. 'In a way, Pop,' I answered casually, knowing it would annoy him.

I turned to Elaine. 'Elaine, this is my father,' I said. 'He's an old man with a very evil mind, but I'm not responsible for it. He had it before I was born.' I spoke across the window to him. 'Pop – Mrs Schuyler.'

Elaine's voice was very rich in the dimness. 'Glad to know you, Mr Rowan.'

Pop's head nodded embarrassedly. Actually, he was very shy when it came to meeting my friends.

'Mrs Schuyler was on the same plane,' I explained. 'I told her I would drop her off at her hotel.'

'Brad is very kind, Mr Rowan.' Elaine kicked the ball further towards the goal. 'I told him not to go out of his way.'

'Bernard is very partial towards women, Mrs Schuyler,' Pop said. 'Especially beautiful women.'

She laughed. 'I can see now where your son inherits his blarney, Mr Rowan.'

'He's a fine lad, Mrs Schuyler,' Pop said, suddenly serious. 'He's got two beautiful children, did he tell you? A boy, almost nineteen, in college, and a daughter in high school.'

I could see her teeth gleam as she smiled. 'I know,' she said.

'He's a good husband and father,' Pop continued. 'He's married to a very fine girl he's known ever since public school.'

I began to squirm in my seat. What had got into the old man, anyhow? 'Cut it, Pop,' I interrupted. 'I'm sure Mrs Schuyler isn't interested in my life story.'

'Please don't, Mr Rowan.' Elaine's voice had a caustic edge to it. 'I'm fascinated.'

That was all he had to hear. From there until we stopped in front of her hotel he kept on talking. Even I had to admit it was a dull story. Who cared right now how bad a student I had been and that I didn't finish high school? I was glad when we finally reached her hotel.

'Wait for me, Pop,' I said taking her bag and jumping out. 'I'll see Mrs Schuyler inside.'

She shook hands with Pop, then followed me through the revolving doors. 'Your father's very proud of you, Brad,' she said as we walked through the lobby.

I stopped in front of the elevators. 'I'm his only child,' I said. 'And he's prejudiced.'

There was a curious smile on her lips. 'He had a right to be. You're quite a guy.' Her voice seemed strained.

I couldn't figure her out, there was something about her that was escaping me. 'Elaine,' I whispered. 'What's wrong?'

'Nothing.' She shook her head. 'Everything.'

'I'll get rid of him,' I said. 'I'll have him take me over to the garage to get my car. I'll tell him I'll drive home.'

'Don't be a fool!' she whispered savagely. 'The only reason he was waiting at the airport was to drive you home. Don't you know that?'

It all added up. He couldn't have known that I told Marge I wouldn't be home until tomorrow because he had spoken to her in the afternoon, and I'd spoken to her in the evening. I should have known that right away because his car didn't swing in from the feed line, but off from the side where he had been waiting.

'I told you we should've stayed there,' I said bitterly.

Her voice was dull. 'It doesn't matter now.'

I looked at her. The shadows of pain had crept back into her eyes and I could feel their hurt inside me. An ache began to throb in my heart. We didn't speak. I could only watch the misery spread its tiny searing threads across her face. The elevator doors opened and she moved towards them.

I handed her the bag. 'I'll call you later,' I said helplessly.

There was a hint of moisture in her eyes. She nodded, not speaking.

'Good night, darling,' I said as the doors closed.

I went back through the lobby and out into the cab.

'Okay, Pop,' I said wearily, settling back into the seat.

He was silent all through the city until we hit the highway. Then Pop looked back at me through the mirror. 'She's a very beautiful lady, Bernard.'

I nodded. 'Yes, Pop.'

'How do you know her?'

Slowly I told him all about her and how I had come to meet her. When I had finished, he shook his head sadly. 'A crying shame.'

With a sense of relief I felt the car swing into our driveway and stop. I didn't want to talk about it any more. I looked at my watch. It was after midnight. 'You might as well spend the night, Pop,' I said. 'It's too late to go home.'

As usual, Pop got independent. 'Nonsense, Bernard. The night is young yet. Me best fares are in front of me.'

As usual, I had to con him. 'Stay, Pop,' I asked. 'This way we can go down together tomorrow. You know how I hate the train.'

Marge was surprised to see me, and I explained to her that the meeting had been called off at the last minute so I had decided to come home. Jeanie came down and we all had coffee in the kitchen. I remember mentioning that I had met Elaine on the plane coming back and seeing the queer look of suspicion on my father's face, but it passed quickly as I told them about Matt Brady's offer.

It was one-thirty in the morning when we were finished and the drug store three blocks away was closed and there was no way I could call Elaine so I went up to bed.

I was restless, and couldn't sleep. I tossed and turned fitfully. Some time during the night, Marge's hand reached out and touched my shoulder.

'Anything wrong, Brad?' Her voice was tender as the night.

'No,' I answered shortly. 'I'm all wound up, I guess.'

'Too much big deal,' she whispered. I heard a rustle of sheets, then she came into my bed. Her arms went around my neck, drawing my head down to her breast. 'Sleep, baby, rest,' she crooned softly as if I were a child.

At first I was tight and tense as a coiled spring, but then slowly everything seeped out of me as I listened to her calm, steady breathing and the warmth of her body crept through me. I closed my eyes.

I called Elaine as soon as I got to the office in the morning. The operator's answer wasn't a surprise to me. Somehow I had known from the moment she had walked into that elevator last night how it would be. And still, I didn't want to believe it. 'What's that?' I asked foolishly, as if I couldn't hear.

The operator's voice was more distinct than ever. There was the professional annoyance with layman in its sound as it came with terrible clarity through the receiver in my ear.

'Mrs Schuyler checked out this morning.'

Chapter FIFTEEN

By three in the afternoon I was in desperation. At first I was angry, then I was hurt. She didn't have to run like that. We were grown people. People fell in love and it was rough, but they didn't run away. There's no place to hide from love.

So I plunged into work. The only way I had to forget. By noon I had everyone in the office crazy. I acted like a demon and I knew it. I didn't even take time for lunch.

But it did no good. The pain kept creeping back inside me until I couldn't stand it any longer.

I chased everybody out of my office and told Mickey I didn't want to be disturbed. I opened a bottle of Scotch and poured me a hooker. Twenty minutes later my head ached as much as my heart.

My private phone began to ring. The one that didn't go through the switchboard. For a long time I sat there listening to it. I didn't want to answer it. Marge was the only one to call me on it and I couldn't talk to her now.

But it kept on ringing and at last I walked across the office to my desk and picked it up. 'Hello,' I grunted.

'Brad?'

My heart began to jump excitedly when I recognised the voice. 'Where are you?' I growled.

'Uncle Matthew's,' she answered.

A sigh of relief escaped my lips. 'I thought you were running away from me,' I said.

'I am,' she answered flatly.

For a moment I couldn't speak, then the pain in my temples bound my head in a vice. 'Why – why?' was all I could ask.

'You're not for me, Brad.' Her voice was so low I could hardly hear her. 'I know that now, especially after last night. I must have been out of my mind.'

'My father's an old man,' I said quickly. 'You don't understand.'

'I understand too well,' she interrupted. 'I only wish I didn't. I don't know why I started with you. There was nothing in it for me in the first place.'

'Elaine!' I could feel the ache searing through me.

'Maybe it was because I was lonely,' she continued as if I hadn't spoken. 'Or maybe because I missed David so.'

116

'That's not true, doll,' I said desperately, 'and you know it.'

Her voice was weary. 'I don't know what's true any more. It doesn't matter, anyway. All I do know is that you're not for me and I'd better run before I get hurt so bad it can never be fixed.'

'But I love you, Elaine,' I protested. 'I love you so much I've been sick ever since this morning when I couldn't get you at the hotel. You're for me like nothing in this world has ever been. When we're together, we're everything a man and a woman are supposed to be to each other. There's never two of us, only one –'

'It's no good, Brad,' her voice cut me off. 'We can't win. There's no way that we can come out even.'

'Elaine,' I called. 'You can't leave me, Elaine!'

'I'm not leaving,' she said quietly. 'It's going to be as if we never met.'

A bitterness ran through me like a flood. 'For you, maybe,' I shouted. 'But not for me. I might as well make believe I've never been born!'

Her voice was deceptively quiet. 'In a way, Brad,' she said, 'that's just the way it will seem.'

I didn't answer. I had no words in me.

'Anyway,' the words were a knife in my heart and her tone twisted it, 'I only called to tell you that Uncle Matt was in New York on business and mentioned that he might drop by your office, if he could find time. Good-bye, Brad.'

The phone went dead in my hand. Slowly I put it down, sank into my chair, and stared across the desk. I felt chill inside me. No more dreams, no more glory, no more ecstasy.

The intercom buzzed and I flipped the switch without

putting the bottle down. 'Mr Brady is here to see you,' Mickey said.

'I can't see him,' I said. 'Send him in to Chris.'

Her voice seemed startled. 'But Mr Rowan –'

'Send him in to Chris!' I shouted. 'I said I can't see him!' I slammed the switch down, cutting her off. For a moment I stared down at the intercom, while the pain inside me rose up and gorged in my throat.

Right behind the pain lay violence. My foot tingled as I kicked my chair across the room. My ears roared as I swept everything off my desk on to the floor.

The door to my office started to open. Quickly I jumped across the room, holding it shut. Mickey's voice came anxiously through it. 'Brad, what's wrong? Are you all right?'

I leaned against the door, breathing heavily. 'I'm all right,' I gasped. 'Go away.'

'But –'

'I'm okay,' I insisted. 'Go away!'

I could hear her footsteps leaving the door, and then the squeak of her chair as she sat down at her desk. Quietly I turned the lock and looked back into my office.

It was a shambles. I tried to care about it but I couldn't. It didn't matter. I took the handkerchief from my breast pocket and wiped my face. I could feel the damp sweat of nausea on my cheeks. I crossed the room and opened the window.

The cold air came running into the room and the nausea went away. For a long time I stood there looking over the city. You're a dope, I told myself. You're acting like a teenage kid. You got everything you ever wanted in this world. Money. Position. Respect. What more do you want? No dame is that important.

That was it. No dame was that important. I knew that

all the time. That's what I always said. I closed the window and walked back through the office. I sat down on the couch and leaned back against the cushions. I was tired and beat so I closed my eyes – and she jumped back into the room.

I could feel the softness of her hair, see the gentle curve of her smile, hear the sweetness in her voice. I rolled over and buried my face in the cushions until I could hardly breathe. But it was no good.

I punched my hand into the cushions to drive her face away. I opened my eyes but she was still in the room, just out of sight.

I got to my feet defiantly. I was shouting now. 'Go away! Don't bother me!' I shut up guiltily as my voice bounded back in the empty room.

Chapter SIXTEEN

As I checked past the desk in my club, I asked the clerk if there had been any calls for me.

He checked the call sheet. 'No, Mr Rowan.'

I went on up to my room. I had told Marge last night that I would be in town late on business and would stay over at the club. I felt dog-tired and beat. I decided to head for the steam room, then get me a rub-down and shower.

I lay flat on the rubbing table while Sam worked out

the kinks in me. I rested my hands on my arms. Sam was a good workman. He had strong, soothing hands and soon I could feel the tension in me easing.

A sharp stinging slap on my rump brought me out of my reverie. 'Your shower's ready now, Mr Rowan,' Sam said.

Lazily I rolled off the rubbing table. 'Thanks, Sam,' I said, stepping into the shower stall. The cold water hit me and I really woke up.

Mickey had a peculiar look on her face when I came in. 'Call Pete Gordy,' she said.

'Get him for me,' I said, going on into my office. I looked around. Yesterday's mess had been cleaned up.

Mickey came in behind me and put some papers on my desk. She turned to walk out without saying a word.

I stopped her. 'Thanks for fixing up, Mickey,' I said.

She stared at me, a puzzled bewilderment on her face. 'What got into you, Brad?' she asked. 'I never saw you like that.'

I shrugged my shoulders. 'I guess I been working too hard,' I answered. 'And it caught up to me.'

I could see she didn't buy my story, but I was the boss so she let it go at that. A few seconds later she had Pete Gordy on the phone.

Pete was one of my best accounts. He owned the largest independent chartered airline in the East. He accounted for about twenty-five per cent of my business.

After the usual greeting I got down to business and asked what I could do for him.

An embarrassed tone crept into his voice. 'Well, Brad,' he said in his best New England twang, 'I don't quite know how to tell you this.'

For a moment I held my breath, then I let it out slowly. I guess he didn't really have to tell me. I had known somehow from the moment I came into the office and got his message. 'What, Pete?' I asked, making my voice flat and blank.

'I'm going to have to pull my account,' he said.

'Why?' I asked. I knew why, but I wanted him to tell me. 'I thought we were doing a hell of a job for you.'

'You are, Brad,' he said quickly. 'I got no beefs there, but –'

'But what?' I insisted.

'Certain things came up,' he said. 'My bankers insisted.'

'What the hell do they care who does your work?' I exploded. 'I always thought you were the kind of guy who ran his own business.'

'Brad, don't make it any tougher for me than it really is,' he pleaded. 'You know how I feel about you. I can't help this thing. I gotta do it or they'll close down my financing.'

My anger left me. In a way he was right. There was nothing he could do about it. Matt Brady had put out the word. Who would dare say no to him?

'Okay, Peter,' I said. 'I understand.'

I put down the phone gently and hit the buzzer. I told Mickey to send Chris in. I spun in my chair and looked out the window. It was hard to believe that one little old man could have so much power.

The intercom squawked. I flipped the switch and Mickey's voice came from it. 'Chris's secretary tells me he left the office before you came in this morning.'

'When will he be back?'

'She didn't know,' came the answer. I turned off the switch. This was great. The house starts tumbling down and the fire chief takes off.

The buzzer rang and I picked up the phone. It was another client. Same story. Sorry, old man. Good-bye. It kept up all day. One after the other called me. I didn't even have time to go to lunch, I was so busy taking cancellations.

By five o'clock the phone had stopped ringing. I looked at my watch gratefully. I was glad the business day was over. Another two hours of this and I would be back in the telephone booth I started from.

I crossed the room to the liquor cabinet and opened it. All the Scotch was gone. I smiled grimly. Mickey had taken no chances when she cleaned the office this morning. I opened the door and looked out on her.

'Where'd you hide the Scotch, baby?' I asked. 'I need a drink.'

She looked up sceptically. 'Brad, you're not going to do that again?'

I shook my head. 'No, baby. I just need a drink.'

She took a bottle from the file cabinet next to her desk and followed me into my office. 'I can use one too,' she said.

I watched her make two, then took the drink she handed me. I sipped it gratefully. 'Hear from Chris yet?' I asked her.

She shook her head. 'I wonder where he is.'

I had an idea. 'Did he see Matt Brady yesterday?' She looked puzzled. 'When I told you to send him in to Chris,' I added.

'Oh – yes,' she remembered.

'For long?' I asked.

'Only a few minutes,' she said. 'Then Mr Brady left.'

'Chris say anything?'

She shook her head. 'Not a word. He left before you. He seemed very nervous.'

I took another pull at my drink. I didn't like the looks of it. Even if Matt Brady did put the word out, how could he get the list of my clients so quickly? He had to have some inside help.

Mickey was watching me. 'What's wrong, Brad? What got into everybody? McCarthy label you Communist?'

I grinned. 'Just as bad,' I said. 'Brady marked me good and proper.'

Chapter SEVENTEEN

I got home for dinner real tired and beat. Marge took one look at my face and steered me to the living-room. 'You better have a cocktail before you eat,' she said quickly. 'You're all wound up.'

I sank into the club chair and looked at her. It was as if I had been away for a long time. There was concern in her eyes but she didn't say a word until after I had sipped the drink.

'What's wrong, Brad?' she asked.

I leaned my head wearily back against the chair. I closed my eyes. 'I got troubles,' I said. 'Brady didn't like the way I talked so he's out to get me.'

'Is that bad?' she asked.

I looked at her. 'Bad enough,' I said. 'I lost about eight of my best accounts today.'

A kind of relief came into her eyes. She sat down on the arm of the chair. 'Is that all?' she asked.

I stared up at her, bewildered. We were going broke and it wasn't important to her. 'Isn't that enough?' I demanded. 'There's nothing worse that could happen.'

She smiled down at me. 'Yes there is,' she said softly. 'Lots worse. And I thought it was happening, too.'

I didn't understand her. 'Like what?'

She took my hand. 'I could lose you,' she said seriously. 'And I thought I was going to, you were acting so strangely. But now I know it was only business. Ever since this steel thing started you haven't been the same.'

I didn't answer.

'That's why you were so upset all the time, why you didn't come home last night. Wasn't it?'

I nodded, not daring to speak. My voice might have betrayed me.

'Poor, tired baby,' she said softly, pressing her lips to my cheek ...'

Jeanie had a date so we had dinner alone. While we ate I told her what had happened during the day. Her eyes were solemn as I spoke.

'What are you going to do now?' she asked when I had finished.

'I don't know,' I answered. 'I'll have to wait and see what happens tomorrow. It all depends on how much business I have left, whether I can keep the agency going.

HAROLD ROBBINS

At any rate, I'll have to start shrinking it soon. We can't afford the payroll the way it is now.'

'You'll have to let some people go?' she asked.

'There's nothing else to do,' I answered.

She was silent for a moment. 'What a shame,' she said softly.

I knew what she was thinking. 'It's not so bad for them, honey,' I said. 'It's not like when I was let out during the depression. There are plenty of jobs now. It's just a shame to break up an outfit like this. It took a long time to build.'

'What did Chris say?' she asked.

I knew she thought a lot of him. I shrugged my shoulders. 'I don't know what he thinks,' I answered. 'I didn't see him all day. He went out early in the day.'

'That's peculiar,' she said. 'Did he know what was going on?'

'I don't know,' I said. 'But I got a hunch that he does.' I explained my suspicions to her.

'I can't believe it!' she exclaimed in horrified tones.

I smiled at her. 'Ambition is a vicious master,' I said. 'It pushes a man in many directions. Some of them are not so nice. It's one of the conditions of society.'

'But no Chris!' she said. 'You've done so much for him.'

'Have I?' I asked. 'Look at it from his viewpoint. He's done so much for me. Now he wants his cut.'

'I can't believe that Chris could be like that,' she insisted.

I pushed my chair back from the table. 'I hope you're right, baby,' I said. 'There's nothing I'd like better to be wrong about.'

I heard the screech of a car stopping in our driveway. 'Who's that, I wonder?' I asked.

'Probably Jeanie coming from her date,' Marge replied.

The door chimes rang. Marge started to her feet. I waved her back. 'Finish your coffee,' I said. 'I'll see who it is.'

I opened the door. Paul Remey stood there. I stared at him in surprise for a moment. 'Paul! What are you doing up here?'

'I had to talk to you,' he said, coming into the foyer. 'Have you gone nuts? What are you trying to do, ruin yourself?'

I took his hat and coat and hung them in the closet. 'We're just having coffee,' I said, evading his question. 'Come and join us.'

He followed me into the dining-room. After greeting Marge, he turned back to me. 'What's this I hear about you fighting with Matt Brady?' he demanded.

'I ain't fighting him,' I said quietly. 'I just turned down a job he offered me, that's all.'

'That isn't what I heard,' he said irately. 'I heard you threw him out of your office.'

'You know me better'n that, Paul,' I said. 'I just don't want to work for him. He came to my office and I didn't see him. I was busy.'

Paul stared at me, his mouth agape. Finally he caught his breath. 'You wouldn't see him,' he said sarcastically. 'One of the five most influential businessmen in the country, and you wouldn't see him. You must be off your rocker. Don't you know that by tomorrow he'll close down your business. Where're your brains, Brad?'

'You're late, Paul,' I said. 'He did a pretty good job on me today. I dropped almost sixty-five per cent of my billings today.'

Paul whistled. 'So fast, eh?'

I nodded. 'How did you hear about it?' I asked.

'Pearson knows I'm a friend of yours,' he said. 'He

called to check on it before he ran the item. I told him I knew nothing about it. That all I knew was your outfit was being considered for the industry public relations plan.'

News travelled fast; the word was out. I slumped back in my chair for a moment. They were right. Who was I to fight Matt Brady? It was like sending a fly out to get an elephant.

He looked over at me. 'What's the story?' he asked.

'Brady wanted me to give the industry committee the go-by and come to work for him. I told him I wasn't interested in working for anybody,' I said in a dull voice.

Weariness crept over me and I closed my eyes. For the first time that day, she jumped before me. Elaine. I could never tell anybody. If I said anything, it would only make it worse. Matt Brady would learn the truth and nothing would stop him then.

Paul was talking. He was trying to figure a way out for me. Nothing he said made much sense though, not even to him. He lapsed into silence after a while and we all sat around glumly.

Suddenly he snapped his fingers. 'I've got it!' he cried. 'Elaine Schuyler!'

I was wide awake now. 'What about her?' I asked.

'She's Matt Brady's favourite niece,' he said. 'I'll ask her to tell him how much you're doing for her.'

I shook my head. 'Nix. I can fight my own battles.'

'Don't be a fool, Brad,' he said. 'She can twist the old man around her finger.'

'I don't give a damn what she can do!' I said, standing up. 'This is my business and Matt Brady's. It's got nothing to do with her and I won't run crying to him behind her skirts.'

'But Brad,' Marge said. 'You're doing so much for her.

You always said, "One hand washes the other".'

'Not this time,' I said. 'I don't want her mixed up in it.'

'But why, Brad?' Marge reproached me gently. 'There's so much at stake. She would be glad to help you. You said you liked her and that she liked you.'

'That's right, Brad,' Paul added. 'Edith said that she never saw Elaine so crazy about anybody.'

I stared at both of them for a second. I tried to speak but I couldn't. The words were stuck in my throat. A wild thought ran through my mind. What was it she had said on that last telephone call. Or was it I who said it? I didn't remember.

It would be like we had never met. What fools we were. How wrong can you be? I found my voice. 'No!' I shouted and stalked from the room.

Chapter EIGHTEEN

A million stars were out, the night was clear and chilly. I sat on the steps and shivered slightly. I dragged on my cigarette, too stubborn to go back inside. Through the brightly lighted dining-room windows I could see Paul and Marge, still at the dining table, talking.

I looked at the house, then down the long driveway through the landscaped gardens to the street. I wondered how long I could hold on to this if I had to close up shop. I totted up my assets. Not too long. Everything I made had gone right back into the business towards expansion.

A car stopped in front of the house. I heard the sound of young voices, then Jeanie's footsteps coming up the walk. She was humming a song lightly. I smiled to myself. The kid knew from nothing. The whole world was her oyster. Better that way.

She stopped short when she saw me sitting there. 'Dad!' she exclaimed. 'What are you doing out here?'

I smiled at her. 'Getting some air, honey,' I answered.

She pecked at my cheek and sat down next to me. 'I didn't tell Mother about her present,' she whispered.

I didn't answer. I had almost forgotten about it. The way things were going now, it didn't look as if I would be able to pick it up anyway.

Bright kid, my daughter. She was quick to sense my mood. 'Is there anything wrong, Dad?' she asked anxiously, peering at my face. 'Have you and Mother had a quarrel?'

I shook my head. 'Nothing like that, honey,' I answered. 'Business problems.'

'Oh.' She didn't sound convinced.

I looked at her. In that moment I knew she was no longer a child. She was a woman, with all the grace and intuition and inscrutability of her sex. 'That's a funny question for you to ask. What made you say that?'

She hedged. 'Nothing,' she answered evasively.

'You must've had a reason,' I insisted.

She didn't look at me. 'You've been acting so queer lately and Mother has been going around with a sad expression.'

I tried to laugh but couldn't. I'd been fooling nobody but myself. 'That's silly,' I said.

Her eyes came back to mine, her hand crept under my arm. She seemed reassured. 'I saw a picture of that Mrs

Schuyler in the paper, Dad,' she said. 'She's very beautiful.'

I played dumb. 'She's all right.'

'Grandpa thinks she's in love with you,' she said.

Silently I swore at him. Pop should have more sense
than to say a thing like that. 'You know him,' I said with
forced lightness. 'He thinks all women are nuts about me.'

A thoughtful look came into her eyes. 'It's possible,
Dad,' she said. 'You're not decrepit, you know.'

I smiled at her. 'Just a little while ago, you said I was
an old fuddy-duddy and not in the least bit romantic.
Remember?'

'But you could fall in love with her,' she insisted.
'Things like that do happen. I saw a picture once where
Clark Gable –'

'That's the movies,' I said, interrupting her. 'And I'm
not Clark Gable.'

'You're better-looking than he is,' she said quickly.

I looked at her sceptically. Her face was serious. I
laughed, a warm feeling inside me. 'Flattery'll get you
nowhere,' I said.

Suddenly she was a child again, with all the romantic
fervour of her age. 'Wouldn't it be terrible, Dad,' she
whispered, 'if she were in love with you and had to go
through life knowing she could never have you?'

An ache, almost forgotten in the last few days, began
to throb again in me. Out of the mouths of babes –

I got to my feet. I had enough. 'Come inside,' I said.
'Uncle Paul's in there and he'd like to see you . . . '

I didn't sleep well. The faint night sounds kept beating
at the windows, but there was no comfort in them for me.
At last the first grey shadows of the coming day crept
into the room. I had found no answers in the night;

perhaps the climbing sun would point out a way. I closed my eyes and dozed . . .

I dropped Paul off at the airport on the way in to the office. He was very glum. 'At least let me speak with her,' he asked before getting on the plane.

I shook my head.

He stared at me for a moment. 'You and your stupid pride,' he muttered, holding out his hand.

I took it, his grip was warm and friendly. His eyes met mine. 'I hope it'll come out right,' he said sincerely.

'It will,' I said more confidently than I felt. 'It has to.'

He turned towards the plane. 'Good luck,' he called back over his shoulder.

'Thanks,' I said. There was a kind of dejection in his walk. Impulsively, I called after him. 'Paul!'

He stopped and turned back to me.

'This is only the first round,' I said, smiling. 'Be brave.'

For a moment there was no expression on his face at all, then he smiled back at me. 'You're nuts,' he said, shaking his head with a half wave of his hand.

Mickey was at her desk her typewriter clacking like mad when I came in. 'Get Chris,' I said.

She nodded towards my office door. 'He's in there waiting for you.'

I lifted a knowing eyebrow. He wasn't wasting any time. I went on through to my office. He was sitting in my chair behind the desk. He was scribbling something on a piece of paper. He looked up as I came in and started to get out of the chair.

I went along with the gag and waved him back into his seat. He watched me curiously. I didn't speak, just sat there, staring back at him.

After a few minutes' silence, he became uncomfortable.

I could see a flush creeping up past his collar. I still didn't speak.

He cleared his throat. 'Brad –'

I smiled at him. 'Comfortable chair, eh, Chris?'

As if touched with a hot iron, he jumped out of it.

I got to my feet, still smiling. 'Why didn't you tell me you were interested in it before, Chris?' I asked gently.

He flushed deeply.

Before he had a chance to speak, I spoke again. 'If you had,' I continued in a still soft voice, walking around the desk and seating myself, 'we might have done something about getting you one just like it.'

He didn't speak; the colour was fading from his face. I could see his control coming back.

'You don't understand, Brad,' he said. 'I'm just trying to help.'

'Who?' I yelled. 'Yourself?'

For the first time since I knew him, I saw him lose control of himself. 'Someone around here has to keep his head on his shoulders!' he shouted back. 'You're dragging this outfit down with you because you don't care about anyone but yourself.'

I began to feel better. Now we were on grounds that I could understand. This pussyfooting, back-stabbing, genteel manner of business never went well with me. On Third Avenue we always settled our quarrels in the open.

'Where in hell were you all day yesterday?' I asked.

'I was trying to keep Matt Brady off our backs,' he said. 'I was at his office. I made a deal with him.'

'What deal?' I asked. 'Almost all our customers are gone and the rest of them are liable to go today.'

He nodded coldly. 'I know,' he said. 'He told me that he would break us the day you wouldn't see him.'

'Who gave him the list of our customers so that he

could go to work so quickly?' I got out of my chair. 'Was that how you figured you could help me? Out?'

His face flushed. 'He wanted some references.'

I smiled. 'That's pretty weak, isn't it, Chris?' I walked around the desk and looked down at him. 'You don't really think I'd buy that, do you?'

He stared up at me. His voice was cold and controlled once more. 'I don't give a damn what you believe,' he said. 'I have a responsibility to all the people working here. I can't stand by and see their work go for nothing.'

'Very noble,' I jeered. 'Judas, too, had a feeling for others. What are your thirty pieces?'

His eyes were bright on mine. I could see the ambitious glitter in them. I knew he felt that I was whipped. 'Brady will lay off if you get out,' he said.

'That silent partner deal you spoke about on the phone?' I asked, pretending an interest.

He shook his head. 'I'm prepared to offer you a fair price for the company. You have to go for everybody's good.'

I sat down again. 'What's a fair price?' I asked.

He hesitated a moment. 'Fifty thousand.'

Big deal. The outfit was netting better than one hundred and fifty grand a year. 'How can you be so generous? I asked sarcastically.

'It *is* generous,' he said doggedly. 'You might as well face it, Brad; you're through here. You haven't enough business left to pay the rent, let alone anything else.'

What he said was true enough, but somehow it didn't matter. If I had to close up shop, I would do it. But I'd be damned if I'd let someone else take what I had built with so much pride and effort.

'Matt Brady agree to finance you?' I asked. 'That's part of the deal too?'

He didn't answer.

I studied him for a minute. He stared back at me. 'Chris,' I said gently.

A faint shadow of triumph flickered into his eyes for a moment as he leaned towards me expectantly.

'I'm almost tempted to take the dough and let you have the outfit.' I spoke quietly. 'But I have a greater responsibility to the people that work here than you. You see, I built this and made their jobs possible. The easiest thing in the world for me to do would be to take your dough and get into something else. I would make out.'

'Sure, Brad,' he said eagerly, rising to the bait. 'You can do anything.'

I let him think he was pushing me in the direction he wanted to go. 'You really think so, Chris?' I asked, as if doubtful.

He was on the hook now and fighting hard to keep it. 'You're one of the best men in the field, Brad,' he said. 'There isn't an outfit that wouldn't give their eye teeth for you to join them. Your record here speaks for itself. Look what you did here with nothing for a start.'

'You've convinced me, Chris,' I said.

He got to his feet, triumph was clear in his eyes now. 'I knew you'd be sensible about it, Brad,' he said, walking around the desk and clapping his hand on my shoulder. 'I told Mr Brady you'd listen to reason.'

I looked at him as if bewildered. 'I think you misunderstand me, Chris.'

His hand fell from my shoulder and his jaw dropped.

'If I'm that good,' I continued, 'I'm staying right here. We'll get over this. My responsibility to the staff is too great to allow me to sell them down the river like slaves.'

'But, Brad,' he said. 'I –'

I cut him off. 'I wouldn't trust you or Matt Brady with

my dog,' I said coldly. 'Much less other human beings.' I punched the buzzer on my desk.

Mickey's voice came from the intercom. 'Yes, Brad.'

'I want the whole staff, down to the office boy, in my office right away,' I said.

'Sure, Brad,' she answered, clicking off.

I turned back to Chris. He was standing there as if he had taken root. 'What are you hanging around for, baby?' I smiled. 'You don't live here any more.'

He started to speak, then changed his mind and started for the door. As he opened the door, I could see that most of the staff was already in Mickey's office, waiting. I had an idea. 'Chris!' I called.

He turned, his hand on the open door.

I spoke loud enough for all of them to hear, I chose my words purely for effect. 'Let my secretary know where to forward your mail. Matt Brady or the devil?' I laughed. 'Seems to me there isn't much choice between them.'

Chapter NINETEEN

I sat at my desk and watched the last of them file from my office. I kept the smile on may face until the door closed behind them. My face ached when the smile went.

It had been a good meeting. I had reviewed the entire affairs briefly from the first meeting with Matt Brady right up to one I had with Chris before they came in. I told them that I could promise them nothing but a fight; that it would not be easy, but if I could count on their support I felt we would make out.

I couldn't lose, especially after letting them hear what I had said to Chris as he went through the door. They promised their co-operation and swarmed around with words of encouragement. Some of them even volunteered temporary salary cuts until we could level off.

I waved that off, leaving the door open if I had to come back to them in the future. Then I shook hands with every one of them and they left.

It was great. I had promised a lot and said nothing. I stared down at the desk dejectedly. The phones were curiously silent. Normally at this time they would be banging like mad. I smiled grimly to myself. There was an old saying in the business – when they stop calling, you're yesterday's news. That's exactly what I felt like.

The intercom buzzed. I flipped the switch lackadaisically. 'Yes?'

'Mrs Schuyler is here and wonders if you'd have time to look at some notes on the Infantile campaign?' Mickey's voice was metallically cheerful.

For a moment I couldn't find my voice. 'Send her in,' I said, closing the switch.

I was on my feet as the door opened. I tried to calm the wild excitement pounding inside me. The door closed behind her.

She stood there looking at me. Her eyes were wide pools of concern; she didn't smile. Then she came slowly towards my desk.

I didn't say a word. I couldn't. There was something about her that belted me where I live. I could feel this woman in every cell of my being.

She looked up at my face. 'You don't look well, Brad,' she said quietly.

I didn't speak, just kept soaking her up with my eyes.

'Aren't you going to say hello?' she asked.

I found my voice. 'Elaine.' I reached for her hand. Just the touch of her fingers made me want more. I started to pull her to me.

She shook her head and slipped her fingers from mine. 'No, Brad,' she said gently. 'It's over. Let's start again.'

'I love you,' I said. 'It's not over.'

'I made a mistake, Brad,' she said in a small voice. 'Please don't keep throwing it up to me. I want to be your friend.'

'You don't love me?' I asked.

I never saw such eyes. They told so much, they held so much pain. 'Let me go, Brad,' she begged. 'Please.'

I took a deep breath and went back to my chair and sat down. With trembling fingers I tapped a cigarette on the desk and lit it. I blew out a cloud of smoke and stared at her through it. 'Why did you come back, Elaine?' I asked. 'To torture me?'

The words seemed to hit her physically. I could almost see her shrink before my eyes. Her voice was tight and strained. 'It's my fault,' she said. 'If it weren't for me, you wouldn't be fighting my uncle.'

'You had nothing to do with it,' I said quickly. 'He doesn't even know I know you.'

'I know about the report he had on you,' she said. 'That's why you didn't want to see him that night. You knew if I went with you, he would know. You were protecting me.'

'I was protecting myself,' I said. 'I was completely selfish about it. Things would have been worse for me the other way.'

She didn't answer.

'How do you know about the report?' I asked, wondering whether Sandra had talked. She knew the name, all right. She could have tied the two together.

'Uncle Matt told me,' she answered. 'He was angry about the way you spoke to him. He felt he was only acting for your own good.'

'Heaven protect me from Matt Brady's good intentions,' I said sarcastically. 'If they were any better, I'd be dead for sure.'

'Uncle Matt felt you would have had a brilliant future with him,' she insisted.

'I had a brilliant future right here,' I pointed out. 'Your dear uncle took care of that. Now I got nothing.' I ground out the cigarette which had burned almost down to my fingers. 'He's a real helpful character,' I added. 'As long as you don't cross him.'

'I can speak to him,' she said.

'No, thanks,' I answered. 'Not interested. It's too late, anyway. He pulled off my best accounts already.' I smiled wryly. 'Your Uncle Matt doesn't waste time.'

'Brad, I'm sorry,' she breathed.

I got to my feet. 'I'm not,' I said. 'Not for myself anyway. You pay for everything you get in this world. You get nothing for nothing. Little happiness – little pain; big happiness – big price. Everything comes out even. The books are always in balance.'

She got to her feet. A cold contempt had crept into her voice. 'You've quit already.'

'What do you mean. I've quit?' I exclaimed in surprise. 'What am I going to do? Sue him.'

Her eyes were cold. 'Uncle Matt will be real disappointed,' she said. 'I got the impression he was looking forward to a fight.'

'What am I gonna fight him with?' I asked. 'Matchsticks? When he cut off my customers, he cut off my dough.'

'I have some money,' she said.

'Save it,' I said tersely.

'I want to help, Brad. Isn't there anything I can do?'

I stared at her and shook my head. 'I don't know, Elaine. I don't know if there's anything anybody can do now. There's an unwritten law in this business, and I broke it. No matter how you feel, the client is always right. Nobody'll come near me now, for fear they might be tarred with the same brush.'

'What about the other members of the Steel Committee? she asked. 'I know some of them. They're still interested in your plan.'

I laughed. 'The way I figure it your uncle probably took care of them too.'

'How do you know unless you try?' she asked. 'I know them pretty well. Most of them have no love for Uncle Matt.'

She had something in her favour. It was worth a chance. I reached for the telephone. 'Who likes him the least?' I asked.

'Richard Martin, at Independent Steel,' she answered, her voice charged with excitement. 'You're going to call him?'

I nodded, asking Mickey to get him for me. I put down the phone while waiting for the call to go through.

'Good,' she smiled, her eyes glowing. 'We've lost too much time already.'

I began to smile. This was a girl after my own heart. Everything she did was for me. Even the way she thought. She took out her cigarette case. The gold gleamed up at me. I walked over and held the light for her. She looked up at me, the blue smoke casting swirling shadows in her eyes.

I grinned down at her. 'If you weren't the woman I love, I'd offer you a partnership.'

'Better be careful,' she warned, smiling slowly. 'I might take you up on it. Then you'd never be rid of me.'

'That's not a bad idea,' I said. 'It ain't me that wants to run away.'

The smile vanished from her lips. 'Can't we be friends, Brad?'

I stared at her so long that she became uncomfortable under my gaze. She looked away from me at the floor. 'Can't we, Brad?' she repeated in a small voice.

'Maybe we can,' I said slowly. 'When love goes.'

She looked up at me. My heart leapt at the sudden hurt in her eyes. I half reached to brush away the pain, but stilled my hand.

The phone buzzed and I went behind my desk and picked it up. Still watching her, I heard Mickey tell me that Martin was out to lunch. I told her to try again and put down the phone.

'He's out to lunch,' I explained.

'Oh.' Her voice was expressionless. She looked down at the floor again.

'Elaine,' I said sharply.

'What?' she asked in the same expressionless voice, still looking down.

'But love's not gone yet, Elaine,' I said and when she looked up at me, I knew she could not hide the truth from me.

The hurt had vanished from her eyes.

Chapter TWENTY

We went to the Colony for lunch. The maître d' picked us up at the door. 'Mr Rowan,' he murmured, 'I have a very choice table for you.'

I looked around. The place was jammed, but this guy was a real smoothie; every table was choice to him. He took us to a table so far away from the front of the restaurant that two more steps and we would have been in Sixtieth Street. I wondered if he had heard the talk about me. I hadn't done this bad since I first came to the place, a young man on the make trying to impress a prospective client.

I was smiling as I sat down. If I remembered right I never got the account.

'What are you smiling at?' Elaine asked.

I told her and she laughed. 'Isn't that ridiculous?'

I shook my head seriously. 'That's the way people live in this town,' I said. 'The word must be out. Rowan's broke.'

We were still laughing when a voice came over my shoulder. 'Elaine Schuyler!' it exclaimed. 'What are you doing in town?'

Resignedly, I got to my feet, a polite smile already on my lips. An attractively youngish middle-aged woman was smiling at us. I let out a silent damn when I recognised her. I should have known better than to come here. She was the society columnist for one of the wire services. We would be in half the newspapers in the country to-morrow morning. It was too juicy an item to miss. Matt Brady's niece and his enemy having lunch.

After a few minutes she went away and I looked over at Elaine. 'You know what this means?' I asked.

She nodded.

'Your uncle will be angry,' I said.

She smiled slowly. 'I don't give a damn.' Her hand rested on mine lightly across the table top. 'I'm with you.'

We went back to the office, and while we waited for my call to go through, she gave me some background on Matt Brady and the steel business. It was quite a story. Those guys really played rough. They made my crowd look like amateurs. It seemed to me there wasn't one among them who hadn't double-crossed the others at least once. Many of them more times than that. It seemed to be their favourite sport.

It was either that or they were so careful about hiding it that they were never caught. No wonder Matt Brady had cautioned me. Willing or not, these boys toed the mark. They took no chances.

My private phone rang and I picked it up. It was Marge. 'How's it going, darling?' she asked.

'Better,' I said, smiling over the phone at Elaine. 'Mrs Schuyler came in this morning. She offered to help and I took her up on it.'

'She's going to speak to her uncle?' Marge asked.

'No,' I answered. 'You know I wouldn't go for that. But we're contacting other members of the committee and she will work with me to get the account in spite of Matt Brady.'

'Oh,' she said disappointedly.

'I'd rather have it that way,' I said quickly.

There was a subtle change in her voice. 'What about Chris?'

Briefly I told her about what had happened that morning. When I had finished there was a silence on the other end of the wire. 'Still there?' I asked anxiously.

Her voice was depressed. 'I'm here,' she said.

'You were so quiet,' I said.

'I just don't know what to say,' she replied. 'I never thought Chris would –'

'Forget him,' I said. 'It's just one of those things. He's no good, that's all.'

'Brad,' she said hesitantly.

'Yes?'

'Maybe it would be better to take his offer. If you don't get the account, we'll have nothing left.'

'Don't be a fool, Marge,' I said. 'If I do take his offer, I'm through anyway. The dough won't last forever and there isn't another place I could go afterwards. Nobody wants a quitter.'

'I had another letter from Brad this morning,' she said, changing the subject.

'Good,' I said. 'What'd he have to say?'

'He thinks the cold is a little better. He has hopes of getting back to classes next week.'

'Wonderful,' I said. 'I told you he'd be all right.'

'I hope so,' she said. 'But I don't know. I'm worried. Nothing seems to be going right.'

'Stop worrying,' I said. 'That doesn't help.'

'I know,' she answered.

'Things'll get worse before they get better.' I tried joking.

It didn't take. 'That's what I'm afraid of,' she said seriously.

'Marge!' I said sharply. I was beginning to lose patience. What had got into her anyway? 'Cut it out!'

'Are you alone?' she asked, her voice changing slightly.

'No.'

'Mrs Schuyler with you?'

'Yes,' I answered shortly.

There was a moment's silence before she spoke. 'Don't forget to tell her how grateful we both are for her help, dear,' she said sarcastically.

The phone went dead in my hand. I looked quickly over at Elaine. She was watching me. I wondered if she could have heard what Marge had said. I played it through.

'Good-bye, dear,' I said into the dead phone and put it down. I turned to Elaine. 'Marge asked me to thank you for your help.'

'Your wife doesn't like me?'

'How can that be?' I smiled awkwardly. 'She doesn't even know you.'

Elaine looked down at her fingers. 'I don't blame her,' she said. 'I'd feel the same way if I were in her place.'

Martin's call came through then, for which I was properly grateful. His voice was cool. He remembered me perfectly. No, he wasn't interested in pursuing the public relations plan any further. Of course he was only speaking for himself, not for the other members of the committee, but he doubted their interest also in view of what happened.

'What happened?' I asked.

His voice was flat and threw cold water on all my hopes. 'Consolidated Steel withdrew from the institute today to pursue their own plan.'

I put down the phone and looked at Elaine. I tried to smile. 'Your uncle is thorough. He pulled Con Steel out of the institute, knowing they wouldn't have enough money to do the job without him.'

She was silent for a moment. 'Brad, you must let me speak to him. He'll listen to me.'

I shook my head wearily. 'Uh-uh. There has to be another way.'

Her voice was depressed. 'What way?'

I leaned back in my chair, 'I don't know,' I said. 'But some where there must be an out.' I looked over at her. 'You were telling me about the steel business and your uncle. Keep talking. Maybe there's something there.'

The day went on while I listened. It was a few minutes after six o'clock when suddenly something she said hit me. I had been sitting with my back to her, looking out at the darkening sky. I spun my chair around.

She had mentioned that her husband had learned something about the way Con Steel had settled its anti-trust case with the Government that he had wanted to discuss with Brady.

'What was it?' I asked.

'I never really knew,' she said. 'David only mentioned it once. He seemed pretty angry about it.'

'Did he speak to your uncle about it?' I asked.

A shadow came into her eyes. 'I don't think so,' she said. 'It was only a few weeks before he got sick.'

I had a hunch. I didn't know what I'd find, but I had to follow this through. I got Paul just before he left his desk in Washington.

I wasted no time on the usual greeting. 'How did Con Steel settle its anti-trust case?'

'By consent decree,' he answered. 'Why?'

'Anything irregular about it?' I asked.

'No,' he answered. 'Usual thing. Con Steel agreed not to interfere with the operations of their competitors.'

'I see,' I answered. 'Who handled the case for the department?'

'I don't know,' he answered. 'But I could find out. Is it important?'

'I got a feeling it is,' I said. 'I hope I'm right. If I'm wrong, I'm dead.'

'I'll call you back in the morning,' he said and hung up.

Elaine was watching me, a look of interest on her face. 'Think you've got something?'

I shook my head. 'I'm only stabbing,' I said. 'But I can't afford to miss a trick. Now tell me everything you can remember about it. Everything your husband may have mentioned.'

The shadow came back into her eyes but she began the whole story over again while I listened carefully.

It was dark when we stepped out on Madison Avenue.

I looked at my watch. Eight-thirty. I took her arm. 'Walk a little?'

She nodded. We had gone almost a block before she spoke. 'What are you thinking, Brad?'

I smiled at her. 'I got a feeling things'll work out,' I lied.

Her hand squeezed my arm. 'Really, Brad? I'm so glad!'

I stopped and looked at her. It was worth the lie to see her eyes glowing. 'I said you were lucky for me, baby.'

The glow went out of her eyes. 'I wasn't the last time, Brad.'

'Last time doesn't count,' I said quickly. 'That had nothing to do with you. This is one that counts. This one you made possible. Without you, I should have no chance at all.'

She didn't answer and we walked silently for a few blocks. The cold night air gave me an appetite. I stopped. 'What about dinner?' I asked. 'I'm starving.'

She looked up at me, her face very still. 'I think we'd better not, Brad.'

I grinned at her. 'What's the matter? Afraid of me? I won't eat you.'

She shook her head. 'It's not that, Brad,' she said earnestly. 'I just think it would be better for both of us, that's all.'

The ache inside me that had vanished all the day she had been with me came back. 'What harm can it do?' I asked angrily. 'You were with me all day and nothing happened.'

Her eyes met mine. Those crazy shadows were dancing deep inside them. 'That's different, Brad. It was business. We have no excuse now.'

'Since when do we need excuses?' I demanded.

She evaded the question. 'Please, Brad,' she said in a low voice. 'Let's not quarrel. Besides, I'm very tired.'

I didn't say another word. I flagged down a cab, dropped her off at her hotel, went on to my garage and then drove home ...

I walked into the house near ten. Marge was reading a paper. I knew she was angry from the way she looked up at me. I bent over the chair to kiss her cheek but she turned her face away.

'Hey!' I protested, a forced levity in my voice. 'Is this the way to greet a weary soldier home from the wars?'

'Wars!' she asked coldly. I didn't like the play she made on the word. It sounded too much like whores. I decided to let it pass.

I mixed myself a little Scotch and water. 'I was working. I think we got an outside chance.'

'We?' she asked sarcastically. 'Who do you mean? Mrs Schuyler and yourself?'

'Wait a minute, Marge,' I said, staring down at her. 'What's eating you anyway?'

'You were too busy, I suppose, making plans with Mrs Schuyler, to call and let me know you weren't coming home for dinner?'

I clapped a hand to my head. 'My God! I forgot.' I smiled down at her. 'Baby, I'm sorry. It's that I had so many things on my mind –'

'You weren't too busy for her. You didn't have too many things on your –'

'Lay off, Marge,' I said angrily. 'Yesterday you were willing for me to ask her help. Today, when she offers it, you're angry. Make up your mind what you want.'

'I don't want anything!' she flared. 'I just don't like the way you're acting.'

I spread my hands helplessly. 'How do you want me to

act?' I asked. 'I'm getting my head kicked in and you're hollering about a phone call!'

She got out of the chair. 'If it's that important to you, then I'm wasting my time,' she said coldly.

This time the fuse really blew. 'What the hell am I?' I yelled. 'A child, that I have to report to you every ten minutes? Leave me alone! I got enough troubles!'

She stood there a moment, the colour draining from her face. Then she turned and went up the stairs to our room without a word.

I puttered around in the living-room a while, had me another drink, then followed her up the stairs. I put my hand on the door to our room and pushed. It didn't move. I turned the knob. It was locked.

I knocked at the door. 'Hey!' I said.

She didn't answer.

I knocked again. Still no sound from inside the room. I stared at the door helplessly, not knowing what to do. It was the first time she had ever locked the door on me.

After a few minutes, during which I began to feel like a fool, I stamped angrily down the hall to the guest room. I spent the night sleeping uncomfortably in my underwear.

Chapter TWENTY-ONE

The razor in the guest room was dull; the water pressure in the shower was uneven and I couldn't get the hot and cold mixed right. I had to dry myself with a small guest towel.

I sucked in my belly and tying the little towel around my waist the best I could, I stalked barefooted through the hall to our bedroom. The room was empty and my clothes weren't laid out on the bed as usual.

I searched through the drawers and closets until I

found a combination of clothing I thought would go well. I dressed quickly and headed down the stairs.

I came into the breakfast nook. My orange juice wasn't on the table and my paper was lying all messed up in front of Marge's chair. I picked up the paper and sat down. I was about to turn to the financial page when my eye caught an item in the society column.

Mrs Hortense (Elaine) Schuyler, niece of Matthew Brady, steel magnate, and prominent in Washington society, has finally crept from her shell after the terrible tragedy of last year. You may remember the tragic loss of her husband and twin children to polio, all within a few weeks. We caught a glimpse of her lunching at The Colony with an attractively rugged man. We checked, and his name is Brad Rowan, prominent public relations counsellor, who is rumoured to be helping her with her Infantile drive. If the life and smile on Elaine's face means anything, we can be sure that work is not the only interest they have in common . . .

The paper had been folded right along that column so I could be sure not to miss it. Annoyed. I turned to the financial page. I could just as well have thrown the paper into the trash, it had no good for me that day. There was a small headline:

CHRISTOPHER PROCTOR APPOINTED SPECIAL ADVISOR ON PUBLIC RELATIONS TO MATTHEW BRADY AT CONSOLIDATED STEEL CORP.

I tossed the paper on the floor. Where was my orange juice? 'Marge!' I called.

The kitchen door opened. Sally's dark face peered through it. 'I didn't heah you come down, Mr Rowan.'

'Where's Mrs Rowan?' I asked.

'She went out,' Sally answered. 'I'll get your juice.' She disappeared into the kitchen.

While I was waiting for the juice, Jeanie came in. There was a mischievous smile on her face. 'If you hurry, Dad,' she said, 'I'll let you drop me off at school.'

I had no patience left. 'Why can't you ride the bus like other kids?' I snapped. 'You too good for them?'

The smile fled from her face. She stared at me for a moment, a hurt expression creeping into her face. There was something there that reminded me of when she was a baby. Without a word, she spun on her heel and left the room.

A second later, I was on my feet and after her. I heard the front door slam. I went to it and opened it. She was hurrying down the driveway.

'Jeanie!' I called after her.

She didn't look back but hurried out of the driveway and was hidden by the big privet hedges around the lawn.

I closed the door and walked slowly back to the breakfast nook. My orange juice was on the table. Absently, I picked it up and sipped it. It didn't taste so good this morning. Nothing was any good this morning.

Sally came in, the eggs steaming golden-yellow, the butter melting on the toast, the bacon crisp and brown. She placed it in front of me and poured some coffee into my cup.

I stared down at it. I remember what I used to say – eggs for breakfast made every day like Sunday. What had gone wrong with me, anyway? I pushed my chair back from the table and got up.

Sally was looking at me, a puzzled expression on her face.

'Don't you feel well, Mr Rowan?' Her voice was concerned.

I looked at her for a moment before I answered. The house seemed curiously cold and empty. As if all love had gone from it. 'I'm not hungry,' I said, walking out of the room.

The morning dragged by. The office was quiet; I didn't have more than four telephone calls all morning. It was almost time for lunch when Elaine called.

Her voice was husky. 'You don't sound right,' she replied. 'Didn't you sleep?'

'I slept,' I answered. I didn't want her to hang up. 'You?'

'I was exhausted,' she said. 'Did you see that item in Nan Page's column this morning?'

'I saw it.'

'Did your wife see it?' she asked.

'I suppose so,' I said. I laughed harshly. 'I didn't see her this morning.'

'Uncle Matt saw it too,' she said. 'He called me. He was very angry. He told me not to see you, that you were nothing but an adventurer.'

I was interested. 'What did you say?'

'I told him I would see whom I pleased,' she said quickly. 'What did you think I would say?'

I ignored the challenge in her voice. I had an idea. 'He was sore, eh?'

'Yes,' she said. 'I never heard him so angry.'

'Good.' I laughed. 'I'll give him a chance to get even angrier. We're going to have an affair.'

Her voice dropped. 'Brad, please. I said it was over. I can't live like that.'

'This is for the newspapers,' I said. 'I want your uncle to get so mad at me that he opens up. He might make a mistake.'

I could hear her draw in her breath. 'I couldn't do that,' she said. 'He's always been so good to me.'

'Okay,' I said, making my voice flat and harsh.

'Brad, please try to understand –'

I cut her off. 'The only thing I know is that you're quitting on me too.' I put false understanding in my voice. 'But it's all right, baby. I don't blame you.'

I could almost feel her wavering over the phone. I kept silent. After a second, she spoke. 'All right, Brad. What do you want me to do?'

I held the feeling of triumph out of my voice while I spoke. 'Get out your prettiest dress. You're giving a cocktail party for the press this afternoon to inform them about your charity drive.'

Her voice was dismayed. 'That too? It's such a cheap thing to do. To take advantage of that horrible –'

I wouldn't let her finish. 'It won't hurt the charity and it will help me. I'll call you back when I've made arrangements.'

I put down the phone and waited a moment, then picked it up again. 'Mrs Schuyler is giving a cocktail party at the Stork at five this afternoon, for the press, in connection with the Infantile drive,' I told Mickey. 'See that all arrangements are made and have the staff get out every columnist in town with photographers.'

I started to put down the phone, then changed my mind. 'Have our own photographer on hand to cover,' I said. 'And keep the swing shift. I want to make the morning papers with this as well as the news services.'

'Okay, boss,' Mickey's voice was crackling. I heard a

buzz through the phone. Then she came back again. 'Paul's on the wire.'

I hit the button on the phone. 'Paul?' I asked. 'You get that dope?'

'Yes,' he said. 'A young chap name of Levi.'

'You know him?' I asked.

'No,' Paul answered. 'He resigned to go into private practice in Wappinger Falls, New York.'

'Wappinger Falls?' I asked. Something about that didn't hit me right. 'Isn't that funny?' Usually when then these guys get a taste of something big they don't go back to the farm. They generally wind up in a cushy job with some big company.

'Nobody seems to know much about him now,' Paul answered. 'But at one time he was considered one of the department's really bright boys. Honour student at Harvard Law and so on. Specialised in corporate anti-trust. This was his first big case.'

'How come he didn't prosecute it?' I asked.

'I don't know,' he said. 'Probably department politics.'

'What's his first name?'

'Robert M. Levi.' His voice was curious. 'You on to something?'

'I'm spitting in the wind,' I said, 'and I hope it blows in Matt Brady's face.'

I put down the phone and hit the buzzer again. Mickey came on. I looked at the clock on my desk. A quarter after one. 'Find out where Wappinger Falls, N.Y., is and how to get there,' I said. 'And call the garage and tell them to have my car ready. Then call home and tell Marge to send my dark blue suit and a complete change, down to the office. Tell her I'll explain later.'

I bolted a sandwich before I picked up the car. I don't

know whether it was the excitement or the sandwich that was tying my stomach into knots, but whatever the reason it was better than the sinking feeling I had had the last few days.

Chapter TWENTY-TWO

I hit Wappinger Falls at two-thirty. It wasn't a very big town; I almost left it at two-thirty-one, but I was lucky. I put on the brakes and skidded to a stop in front of a row of stores.

I got out of the car and looked down the street. There were a few office buildings there, two-storey taxpayers. I quickly checked the directory in each. There was no Robert M. Levi listed.

I went back out into the street and scratched my head.

This was the last place in the world I would ever expect a promising young corporation lawyer to settle down to practice. I saw a cop walking down the street. I went to meet him.

'Officer,' I said, 'can you help me out? I'm looking for someone.'

Long ago I had found out that upstate New Yorkers were even more taciturn than New Englanders. This cop wasn't going to prove me wrong. He pushed his cap back on his head and surveyed me slowly from head to foot. Then he spoke, or rather grunted. 'Hmmm?'

'I'm looking for a lawyer, Robert M. Levi.'

He stood there silently for a minute while he thought it over. 'There's no lawyer aroun' here by that name.'

'There must be,' I said. 'I was told in Washington that he was here. I drove up from New York to see him.'

'You mean the city,' he said.

'Yes,' I answered. 'New York city.'

'Hmmm,' he said. 'Nice day for a drive.' He shifted a wad of tobacco around in his mouth and spat carefully into the gutter. 'What you lookin' for this fellow for?' he asked.

I had a hunch he knew where Levi was, so I told him the best thing that could come to mind. 'I got a job for him. A good one.'

His eyes looked at me shrewdly. 'There's a lawyer shortage in the city?'

'No,' I answered, 'but Levi's got the reputation of being one of the best young men in his line.'

He glanced down the street at my car, and then back at me. 'There's no lawyer by that name practisin' here, but there's a Bob Levi aroun'. He was a flyer durin' the war. An Ace – got eleven Jap planes. Heard he spent

HAROLD ROBBINS

some time in Washington after the war. Might he be the one?'

That was good enough for me. 'Yes,' I said quickly, 'he's the one.' I lit a cigarette. This Levi must be quite a guy. The more I heard about him, the less I could believe that he would settle down here. 'Where can I find him?'

The cop raised his arm and pointed up the street. 'See that corner there?' I nodded and he continued. 'Well, you turn there an' follow it to the end of the road an' that's it. You'll see a sign there, Krystal Kennels. He'll be there.'

I thanked him and got back into my car. I turned at the corner he had pointed out. It was a dirt road. I followed it for a mile and a half. At last when I was beginning to think I was the victim of a practical joke, the breeze brought the sound of barking dogs to my ear and just around a turn the road came abruptly to an end.

There was the white sign, Krystal Kennels. Underneath it were the words: 'Wire Fox Terriers – Welsh Terriers. Puppies available. Mr and Mrs Bob Levi, Props.'

I got out of the car and walked up to a small white cottage, set back from the road. Around behind the house I could see the wire fences of the kennels and hear the happy yapping of the dogs. A Ford station wagon stood beside the house. It was a forty-nine car. I pressed the bell.

I could hear it ring in the house and at the same time I heard a bell ring out in the kennels. It seemed to be a signal that set all the dogs to barking. Through the din I could hear a man's voice.

'Out in the back here,' it called.

I came down off the steps and walked around the house towards the kennels. The walk was neatly kept, the grass freshly cut, the flower beds trimmed and the earth beneath them just turned.

'Over here,' the voice called.

I peered through the wire fence. A man was sitting on the ground tending to a small dog that a woman was holding. 'Be with you in a minute,' he said in a pleasant voice, without looking up. The woman smiled at me without speaking.

I leaned on the fence and watched them. He was cleaning the dog's ears with a long swab. His eyes squinted in concentration. After a minute, he grunted and got to his feet. The woman let the dog go and he scampered happily off in the direction of his playmates.

'Had a bug in his ear,' the man explained, looking at me. 'Gotta keep 'em clean or there's no telling what might happen.'

I smiled at him. 'People get bugs in their ears too,' I said. 'But when they do, it generally does no good to clean their ears. It's their mouths that need washing.'

A quick light of caution jumped into the man's eyes. He cast a side glance at the woman. She didn't speak. I looked at her. For the first time I noticed a certain Oriental cast to her features.

'What can I do for you, sir?' he asked. I noticed his voice had gone flat and expressionless. 'Looking for a puppy?'

I shook my head. 'No. I'm looking for a Robert M. Levi. He was an attorney for the Department of Justice in Washington. You're the only one by that name out here. Are you the man?'

Again that glance flashed between them. The woman spoke. 'I'd better get up to the house. I've work to do.'

I stepped aside and let her through the gate. I watched her go up the walk. There was a certain Oriental manner about the way she walked too – short, careful steps. I turned back to the man and waited for him to speak.

His eyes were on her until she disappeared into the house. There was a look of pain in them that was strange to see. He turned back to me, a veil dropping over them, hiding whatever he felt. 'Why do you ask, mister?'

I didn't know what was torturing this guy, but I didn't want any part in prolonging it. There was something about him that I liked. 'I'm looking for some information and advice,' I said.

He looked around me at my car and then back at me. 'I gave up the practice of law several years ago, sir,' he said. 'I'm afraid I can't be of much help to you.'

'It's not law that I'm interested in,' I said. 'It's history.'

He looked puzzled.

'About a case you worked on for the government,' I explained. 'Con Steel. It was an anti-trust matter.' I lit a cigarette, watching him carefully. 'I understand you investigated and prepared it.'

The suspicious look came back into his eyes. 'What have you got to do with it?' he asked.

'Nothing, really,' I said. 'It just may be pertinent to a matter I'm working on, so I thought I'd come and see you.'

'Are you a lawyer?' he asked.

I shook my head. A hunch told me I'd better go careful with this guy or he'd clam up altogether. 'I'm a public relations counsellor,' I said, taking out a card and handing it to him.

He looked at it carefully, then gave it back to me. 'Why are you interested in that case, Mr Rowan?' he asked.

I played a long shot. 'I spent eight years building up the business you see on that card. Eight years of work and all my life before getting ready for it.'

I dragged on the butt watching his face. A look of interest began to show there. I kept on going. 'One day

169

I'm tipped off to the big deal, representing the whole industry. I made my pitch and I sell. I know I got it in my pocket. Then a guy calls me down to his office and offers me a job. Sixty grand a year. Big money. I can buy everything I want in this world. There's only one hitch.'

I stopped again to see if I had him with me. He was with me, all right. 'What's that?' he asked.

I dragged on the butt and spoke slowly, 'All I gotta do is doublecross everybody else in the deal. Dump all the people who work for me and helped make a shot like this possible, and toss over my friends.'

I ground the cigarette under my foot 'I told this guy the only thing I could. To keep his job. That was just a few days ago.

'Today I'm busted and almost beat. I dropped eighty per cent of my business all because he put me on his D.D. list. I came up here on a hunch, grabbing at a straw. While I stood here talking to you, I got a feeling that something like what's happening to me, once happened to you. That same guy did it. Want to know his name?'

There was a far-away look in his eyes as he answered. 'You don't have to tell me. I already know his name.' I could see him take a deep breath. His voice was as filled with hatred as any human sound could be. 'Matt Brady.'

'Give the man sixty-four silver dollars,' I said softly. 'Now where are you going to spend it?'

His eyes came back from space and fixed on mine. 'It's hot out here in the sun, Mr Rowan,' he said. 'Why don't you come on up to the house and we can talk. My wife makes a nice cup of coffee.'

Chapter TWENTY-THREE

His wife's coffee was all that he claimed it to be. It was
hot and black and heavy, but clear, not muddy like many
strong coffees. We sat in the kitchen, with a cool breeze
coming from the open windows, and talked.

His wife was Eurasian. Half German, half Japanese.
He had met her in Tokyo while with the occupation
forces, and she had a strange combination of beauty.
Almond eyes, but blue; thick black hair that fell in soft

waves down past her high cheekbones to her delicate throat.

They listened attentively while I told them the story of my relationship with Matt Brady. When I had finished they exchanged a curious glance.

Levi's face was impassive when he spoke. 'Just how do you think we might be able to help you, Mr Rowan?'

I held my hands open in front of me in a gesture of helplessness. 'I don't know,' I confessed. 'I'm stabbing in hopes that I'll find something.'

He stared at me silently for a moment, then his glance lowered to the coffee in front of him. 'I hate to disappoint you, Mr Rowan,' he said softly. 'But I can't think of a thing.'

I had the feeling he wasn't telling all the truth. He had been too interested when I mentioned Brady. There had been too much hatred in his voice. He was afraid of something. I didn't know what it was, but I was sure of it. Then it clicked. Everything began to fall in place. Brady had something on him.

Somewhere in the course of his investigation into Con Street he must have come too close for Brady's comfort. An idea of what Brady might do in a case like that came over me. He would find the man's weak spot, then hammer at it until the guy folded. He was doing it to me; he could have done it to Levi. What other reason would a man like him have to make him suddenly abandon a promising career and settle down to something as alien to his ability and training as this?

'There must be something,' I insisted. 'You worked on the Con Steel case. I was told you know more about that outfit than any man alive, except Matt Brady.'

Again that curious glance between his wife and himself.

'I'm afraid there's nothing I know that would be of help to you,' he said equally stubborn.

I could feel a weary hopelessness as I got to my feet. Nothing but blanks everywhere. Apparently I was dead and refused to admit it. My mouth twisted in a bitter smile. 'He's got you too,' I said.

Levi didn't answer, just looked up at me through inscrutable eyes.

I stopped in the doorway and looked back. 'Need a partner here?' I asked sarcastically. 'Or does Matt Brady supply the dogs when he throws you to them?'

A flash of fire showed in his eyes. 'The dogs are my idea,' he flared. 'They're better than people. They don't know the meaning of betrayal.'

I went out the door and down the long neat walk to my car and headed back to town. I was about halfway back to the main road when I heard a horn honk at me. I looked up in the mirror. Levi's wife was driving the station wagon I had seen in the driveway. I pulled in to the right to let her pass.

She shot past me in a cloud of dust and around a curve in front of me. The station wagon was parked on the side of the road and she was standing beside it, waving at me. I pulled to a stop beside her.

'Mr Rowan,' she said in that curious accent. 'I must talk with you.'

I pushed open the door on her side. 'Yes, Mrs Levi?'

She climbed into the car and nervously lighted a cigarette. 'My husband wants to help you, but he's afraid,' she said quickly. 'He's afraid you are another Brady man.'

I laughed shortly.

'Do not laugh, Mr Rowan,' she said. 'It's not fawny.'

The laughter died away in my throat. It certainly wasn't funny. Only a fool laughed at a funeral. And it was even worse when the funeral was your own. 'I'm sorry, Mrs Levi,' I apologised. 'I didn't mean it that way.'

She glanced at me out of the corners of her eyes. 'There are many things my husband would tell you but he dare not.'

'Why?' I asked. 'What could Matt Brady do to him now?'

'It's not for himself Bob is concairn,' she answered. 'It is for me that he is afraid.'

I didn't get it. What could Matt Brady have to do with her? It must have shown in my eyes.

'Can I talk to you?' she asked, a certain pleading in her voice.

It was more than just her words I heard. It was many things she said all at once. Are you my friend? Can I trust you? Will you harm us? I thought of all these things before I answered. 'You may know a person all your life and never really know what he is like,' I said carefully. 'Then something happens and you find that all the people you knew are like nothing and someone you never saw before will reach out a hand to help. That's the way it is for me right now. No one I know can help me.'

She drew on her cigarette, her strange blue eyes looking far down the road through the windshield. After a while she began to speak softly. 'When I first met Bob Levi, he was a bright, laughing young man, always with a smile and eye for the future. He had high hopes and ambitions.'

The cigarette was short in her fingers and she tapped it out in the ashtray on the dash. There was a note of sorrow in the sound of her voice now. 'It has been many seasons since I saw him smile. His ambitions are no more, and it has been as long and troubled for me as it has for him.'

Her strange eyes looked up at mine. 'We have a saying

in my country – there is no sorrow that love does not precede. It is so. For our love, because of me, my husband must spend his days in exile.'

She reached for another cigarette. I took one and held a match for her. I didn't speak.

She kept watching me until my cigarette was glowing. 'So you see why he dare not speak,' she said. 'I would not care for you to think he was a coward.'

'I didn't think that,' I said. 'But why couldn't he say something?'

'Matt Brady is a terrible man,' she said slowly. 'He found out that Bob brought me to this country illegally. His detectives could not find anything about Bob so they found out about me. All Bob wanted was for us to be together after he returned, so he bought a Shanghai visa and false papers and I came in that way.

'We were happy together until Mr Brady's detective told Bob that he knew what had happened and that if Bob did not lay off he would inform the authorities. Bob did the only thing he could. He quit. It was better to him that way than for me to go back to Japan.'

I remembered what Paul had told me about the Con Steel case. It had been settled by a consent decree after Levi had quit the department. Without him the case had fallen apart at the seams. Matt Brady must have been real proud of himself.

I didn't know what to say. These poor people had gone through enough. There was no point in my adding to their troubles. I kept quiet, letting the smoke drift idly out of my nostrils.

Her voice caught at my ear. 'My husband is not happy, Mr Rowan.'

I looked at her, startled.

'Every day I watch him die in little pieces,' she said.

'He is a man working like a boy.'

I knew what she meant but didn't know what she was getting at. 'What can I do to help, Mrs Levi?' I asked helplessly. 'I'm practically at the end of my own rope.'

'Bob knows more about Matt Brady, business and personal, than anybody else in the world,' she said, watching my face. 'If you would give him a job, he would be of real help to you.'

'He could have a job in a minute,' I protested. 'But I can't shove it down his throat. You just told me why.'

She looked down at her cigarette. 'He does not know that I came after you. I told him I was going to market. I will return and tell him that I spoke with you and told you the truth. Then he will go to you.'

'Do you think he will?' I asked, a faint hope stirring inside me once more.

She got out of the car and stood there in the country road, the wind blowing her hair about her face. 'I will make him go, Mr Rowan,' she said softly. 'No matter what it costs. It is not pleasant to be the instrument of your husband's death.'

I watched her get into the station wagon and make a U turn in front of me. I could see the painted letters, Krystal Kennels, as she passed me, going back. She waved her hand but there was no smile on her face. Only a look of tense concentration.

I looked up in the rear-view mirror. The station wagon was almost hidden in the cloud of dust behind it, then it disappeared around the curve and was gone.

I looked at the clock on the dash. It was almost four. I turned the key and pushed in the starter. With an almost silent hum, the big motor started. I put the car in gear and began to roll. I would have to make time if I were to be at Elaine's cocktail party at five o'clock.

Chapter TWENTY-FOUR

Say something nice about somebody and nobody will listen. Make it mean, malicious, scandalous and everybody in town will help you spread the word. Within three days we were an item in every major column in the papers from coast to coast. Our pictures were in every yellow rag that had the space to print them.

In four days we were the town's biggest romance, the hottest affair. For all I knew we might even have made the Sightseer's guide. We were seen at the latest shows, the most fashionable restaurants. Heads would turn to watch us as we walked by, mouths would gape, people would whisper, their knowing chuckles following us.

But the kid was great. She kept her eyes front and her head up. If she heard the talk, she didn't show it. If it hurt her, she never let me see it. The more I saw of her, the better I liked her.

I tried to explain to Marge what I was doing, but after that fight she wouldn't listen. Even Jeanie looked at me cross-eyed. They both made like they didn't know I was alive. Even my father didn't buy my story.

The papers had done too good a job. They got to everybody except the man they were supposed to reach. Each morning we asked each other the same question. 'Did you hear from Matt Brady?' And each morning the answer was the same. 'No.'

But on Wednesday morning when I got her on the phone, I got my first break.

'Aunt Nora called me,' she said.

'Who's she?' I asked.

Her voice was surprised. 'Uncle Matthew's wife.'

'I didn't even know he was married,' I said. 'I never heard a word about her.'

'You wouldn't,' she explained. 'Aunt Nora's an invalid. She's been in a wheelchair for almost forty years now. She almost never leaves the house.'

'How come?' I asked. 'What happened to her?'

'Her legs and hips were smashed in an automobile accident a year after they were married,' she answered. 'Uncle Matt was driving a new Stutz and it turned over. He was thrown clear but she was pinned beneath it. He's never forgiven himself for that.'

'It's good to know he has some human feelings,' I said

callously. 'I was beginning to give up hope that I would ever find any.'

'Brad, don't be vicious,' she said reproachfully. 'It's a terrible thing. Aunt Nora was only a young girl then. Nineteen, I think.'

I paused. 'What did she want?' I asked.

'She thought it might be a good idea for me to come down and visit,' Elaine answered. 'She was disturbed by everything she read in the papers.'

'Did Uncle Matt have anything to say?' I asked.

'She said he had been very angry about it at breakfast but said that he had warned me once and that was all. That's why she decided to call me.'

'Good,' I said. 'Don't go. Let him boil.'

She hesitated. 'Brad, are you sure we're doing right? I don't see where it's helping.'

'I don't know,' I answered. 'I told you it was only a long shot anyway. All I'm trying to do is loosen him up a little and hope that he'll slip somewhere.'

'Okay, Brad,' she answered. 'I'll call Aunt Nora and tell her.'

'We have a lunch date,' I reminded her.

'I know,' she said. 'Aren't you getting a little tired of the act?'

'Who's acting?' I smiled into the phone.

Her voice grew soft. 'I said no more, Brad. We have an understanding about that, remember?'

'All I know is that I'm with you,' I said. 'When I'm with you, nothing else matters. Business, money, Matt Brady, nothing.'

'Nothing, Brad?' her voice was softly questioning. 'Your family?'

I closed my eyes. I hesitated a moment.

'Don't answer, Brad,' she said quickly. 'I wasn't being fair.'

The phone went dead in my hand and slowly I put it down. She didn't want me to answer. I wondered if she was afraid of what I might say. The intercom buzzed. I flipped the switch.

'Mr Robert M. Levi to see you,' Mickey's voice crackled.

I had almost given up on him. I should have known better than to think a woman like his wife would miss – not after having seen that look on her face as she drove off. 'Send him in,' I said and turned to face the door.

If he hadn't been announced I would never have taken him for the same guy I had seen up in Wappinger Falls. He was wearing a dark grey suit, white shirt and maroon tie. His face was tanned from the sun and there were tiny squint wrinkles in the corners of his brown eyes. I got to my feet.

There was a warm smile on his lips. 'I would have come in on Monday,' he said. 'But all my suits were too big for me. I had to get a tailor to take them in.'

'The investment may never pay off,' I said.

His gaze wandered slowly around my office, and finally came back to me. He took out a cigarette and held a match to it. 'I'll take a chance on that,' he said. 'That is, if your offer's still good.'

I liked him. This was a bright smart guy. But he had something else about him that I liked even more. There was a quality of decency in the set of his mouth and chin. You would never have to lose any sleep worrying about this guy when your back was turned. I stuck out my hand.

'Welcome to the big city, farmer,' I said.

He grinned as he took my hand. 'By cracky,' he said in

as good an imitation of an upstate twang as I ever heard. 'You got mighty fair diggin's here.'

His grip was firm and solid. From the moment our hands touched I knew we would be friends. I think he knew it too. 'Where do I hang my hat?' he asked.

It was my turn to surprise him. I hit the buzzer on my desk Mickey's voice came through the box. 'Yes, boss?'

'Everything ready?' I asked.

'All set, boss.' There was a smile in her voice.

I beckoned him to follow me and went out into the corridor to the office next to mine. I stopped in front of Chris's old office and waited for him to catch up to me. I gestured at the door.

He stared at it for a moment and then turned to me. He gulped and finally spoke. 'My name's on the door already.'

I nodded. 'Been there since I got back that day.'

'But – but how'd you know I'd come?' he managed to ask.

'I was getting a bit worried,' I admitted smiling. 'The office looked so good I wanted you to see it before we had to close down the place.'

He raised a quizzical eyebrow. 'It's that bad, eh?'

I held the door open for him. 'Pretty rough,' I answered, following him into his office. 'Our mutual friend has done a pretty good job up to now. He's ahead on all score cards.'

He walked around behind his desk and sat down. I could see his fingers resting lightly on the polished wood of the desk. There was something almost loving in their touch.

'Hilde's waiting in the station wagon downstairs,' he said. 'I brought down a batch of my records on Brady and the Con Steel case with me. I thought they might come in handy.'

'Good,' I said. 'We'll send a boy down after them.'

A kind of disappointment flashed across his face. I caught on quickly. 'Then I'll call my garage and have them send a man around for the car,' I added. 'That way she'll have time to come up and see the office.'

I walked to the door. I'll give you time to get used to the place,' I said. 'After lunch we'll have a staff meeting and you'll meet the gang. Then we'll settle down and see where we go from here.'

He got up behind his desk. 'Thanks, Brad,' he said earnestly. 'I don't know anything about this business but I hope I'll be of help.'

'Just your being here is a help,' I said. 'Not many guys would jump on to a sinking ship.'

Chapter TWENTY-FIVE

I learned more about Con Steel that afternoon than I had learned in all the last few weeks. But there was nothing there that I could put a finger on. Matt Brady had been too smart.

It was almost seven o'clock when I leaned back in my chair wearily and rubbed my eyes. I pushed the stack of papers on my desk to one side and looked over at Bob. 'I've had it, kid,' I said. 'My head's spinning. We better pick up in the morning.'

He looked at me, smiling. He seemed as fresh as when he came in that afternoon. I envied his youth. 'Okay, Brad,' he said, getting to his feet.

The telephone rang and I picked it up automatically. 'Yes.'

'Mr Rowan?' The voice was female, questioning and vaguely familiar but I was too beat to place it.

'Speaking,' I answered.

'This is Sandra Wallace,' she said.

I forced a smile into my voice. 'Sandy, it's good to hear from you.'

She wasted no time. 'I want to see you Brad.'

I closed my eyes and leaned over the desk. This was no time for romance. I was too tired. Besides, if she didn't know the score by now, the game wasn't for her. 'I'm pretty jammed,' I said. 'I can't get down there just now.'

'I'm in the drugstore in your building,' she said.

I was beginning to sharpen up. This was no passion call. 'Come on up then,' I said. 'Don't be so damned formal.'

I could hear her laugh as she hung up the phone. Bob was looking at me with a curious look in his eyes. I put down the telephone. 'Maybe tomorrow will be better,' I said.

He didn't answer, just nodded and started for the door. Halfway to it, he stopped and turned back to me.

'Yes, Bob?' I asked.

'Tell me if I'm out of line,' he said. 'But there's something I don't get.'

'What?' I asked.

His face flushed. 'This stuff in the papers about you and that Schuyler dame.'

He didn't have to say any more. I knew what he meant. 'I'm not trying to crawl, if that's what you mean.' I got to my feet. 'Elaine is an old friend. She's on our side.'

'I suppose you know what you're doing,' he said. I could tell from his voice that to him the story didn't altogether make sense.

For the first time I began to feel that maybe it hadn't been too good an idea. Marge and my old man might be prejudiced, but this guy had nothing to gain from what he said. It was a completely outside point of view. 'I had to try something,' I said weakly.

His voice softened but didn't altogether lose that quality of scepticism. 'I met her several times in Washington. She's one of the most attractive women I ever saw.'

The words were out of my mouth before I could stop them. 'She's as good as she looks.'

A flash of understanding glowed for a moment in his eyes, then he quickly turned away. 'I'll see you in the morning, Brad,' he said, reaching for the door.

It opened before he could touch it. Sandra stood there. 'Oh, I'm sorry!' she exclaimed. 'I didn't mean to interrupt.'

'It's okay, Sandy,' I said. 'Come on in.'

'I was just leaving,' he explained. 'Good night, Brad.' The door closed behind him as I came around the desk.

'Good to see you, Sandy,' I said, taking her hand.

She smiled. 'You didn't sound happy over the phone.'

'I was tired,' I said, steering her to a chair. 'Your boss is doing a good job of kicking my teeth in.'

'My ex-boss, you mean,' she said. 'I'm looking for that help you promised.'

I was surprised, and showed it. 'You finally quit?'

'Tomorrow,' she answered. 'He doesn't know it yet.'

'What made you change your mind?' I asked. 'I thought you could take it.'

'You did,' she said. Her eyes looked into mine. 'I know

185

I haven't got the chance of a snowball in hell with you. But I can't sit in that office all day and help him.'

It wasn't often in my life that I felt humble. But I was humble before the honesty of her glance. 'You're very kind,' I said.

She got to her feet and came towards me, her eyes still on mine. 'When I left you that day I told myself that it was over, that there was nothing you had for me. You belonged somewhere else. But when the day went by and I saw what was happening, and knew each time he hurt you, I hurt with you, I made up my mind.'

I didn't speak. She was very close to me now and I could sense the urgency in her body, the purely animal sexuality she had for me. I fought the pull and waited.

'You may have nothing for me, but I have a feeling about you. I've known enough men to know what I'm saying. No one ever made me feel the way you do; no one ever can.'

'You're young,' I said huskily. 'Some day a guy will show who's just for you. Then I'll be like nothing in his shadow.'

A faint smile crossed her lips. 'I'll believe it when I see it.'

I turned and went back around my desk. I lit a cigarette. 'You're really leaving him?' I asked.

She was still watching me. She nodded. 'Believe me?'

I had no answer.

She returned to her chair. 'You said you would get me a job.'

I hesitated.

'Were you lying?' she asked quickly.

I shook my head. 'I was a lot more cocky then. I didn't know what Matt Brady could do.'

'Then you won't help me?'

186

'I didn't say that,' I protested. 'I just don't know whether I have enough friends left who will listen.'

'But you'll try?' Her eyes were still on my face.

'I'll try like crazy,' I said.

She got to her feet. 'That's all I ask,' she said. She looked at her watch. 'There's a plane back in an hour. I'll just make it.'

I came around the desk. 'You'll call me Monday?'

'I'll call you.' She held out her hand to me.

I took it and looked down at it. 'Sandy,' I said. 'I'm sorry if I'm not all the man you think I am. I didn't mean to make promises I couldn't keep.'

She forced a smile to her lips. 'You're enough men for me.'

I looked into her eyes. There was no deceit there. 'Thanks, Sandy.'

Her lower lip trembled and I pulled her towards me. I kissed her.

'Brad!' Her head drew back. She held my face close to her while her eyes searched mine silently.

'Sandy, I'm sorry,' I whispered.

Her lips parted as if she were about to speak. There was a sound behind us, then another voice.

'Brad, you've been working too hard, so I came down to get you!' The door finished its opening swing and Elaine stood there.

For a moment we were too startled to move, then Sandy's arms dropped from around my neck.

The smile froze on Elaine's face, then slowly disappeared as hurt crept up into her eyes. She stood very still and small in the doorway, her hand on the doorknob as if to hold herself erect. Her gaze went from me to Sandy and back. At last she spoke.

'Hello, Sandra.' I could hear her fighting to control her voice.

'Mrs Schuyler,' Sandy said huskily.

There was a veil over Elaine's eyes now that locked me out. 'Maybe I was wrong, Brad,' she said, the hurt finally seeping through to her voice. 'But I didn't believe you when you said you were going to play all the angles. Now I know better!'

The door slammed and she was gone. Sandy and I stared at one another. It was as if a spell had broken. I ran to the door and opened it. The office was empty.

'Elaine!' I called and ran out into the corridor. I heard the click of the elevator doors. 'Elaine!' I called again and ran towards them.

It was too late. The corridor was empty. I stared helplessly at the closed doors, then turned and slowly walked into the office.

Sandra was standing there watching me. I walked past her and sank miserably into my chair. 'You love her very much, Brad,' she said.

I nodded.

She walked to the door and opened it. 'Good night, Brad,' she said.

'Good night,' I answered. The door closed and I didn't look up. I leaned back in the chair and closed my eyes. I could feel the pain that showed in Elaine's eyes. Everything inside me hurt with her. Nothing was right. Nothing would ever be right again. Except Matt Brady.

He had won. I had no stomach left for the fight. I looked around the office. It had been great while it lasted, but the party was over. There was nothing left to do but to pay the piper. Tomorrow I would close up the place and next week I would go out and look for a job.

I crossed the office, looking for a bottle. Might as well

do things in style. The liquor was better off inside me than inside my creditors. I was just pouring myself a drink when there was a soft knock at the door.

'Still there, Brad?' Levi's voice called.

'Come in, Bob,' I answered. I smiled bitterly to myself. Might as well face him now. It wouldn't be any easier to tell him in the morning. He just had the shortest job on record.

There was a look of excitement on his face. He leaned over my desk. 'What have you got to do with Matt Brady's daughter?' he asked.

I stared up at him in bewilderment, the drink still in my hand. He was even more mixed up than I. 'Mrs Schulyer is Brady's niece,' I said.

'I'm not talking about Mrs Schuyler,' he said impatiently.

'Then who are you talking about?' I asked.

My drink slopped all over the desk when I heard his answer. Some of it even ran down on my trousers but I didn't give a damn. I just came back from the graveyard.

'Sandra Wallace,' he answered.

Chapter TWENTY-SIX

I should have figured something like that before, but my head wasn't on straight. I was like the bookie who had gone legit after many years. It was a new kick and he never figured there was larceny in the business world. So he ran so straight that before he knew it he lost his stake and had to go back across the tracks. That was me.

I had been too impressed with the surface. These babies were no different from anybody else. They only buried their dirt deeper and you had to scratch harder to dig it up.

'Got the proof?' I asked, wiping the liquor off my trousers.

He shook his head. 'I never really went after it. It was only an accident that I came across it, and it had nothing to do with the government's case, so I left it alone.'

'It might have saved your job,' I said. I didn't understand why he hadn't used that dope before.

He looked at me steadily. 'It wouldn't have kept Hilde here.' He took out a cigarette. 'Seeing her here in your office brought it all back. I thought maybe you found out too.'

'What about Sandy?' I asked. 'Does she know?'

'No,' he answered. 'Nobody knows except her parents. As I understand it, her father is dead. It leaves only her mother to prove our story and I doubt that she'll talk.'

I lit the cigarette he still held in his hand. I was wide awake now. The wheels were churning inside my head. I poured two drinks and held one towards him. 'Let's have the story from the beginning,' I told him.

He took the drink and settled in the chair across from me. 'I was checking Con Steel's common stock list. From 1912, when Matt Brady transferred some shares to his new bride, until 1925, he never sold or transferred another share. Only added to his holdings as he exercised various warrants or options. But in Twenty-five he transferred five hundred shares to Joseph and Marta Wolenciwicz in trust for Alexandra Wolenciwicz. These shares were to be held in trust until his death; then they were to be turned over to Alexandra.'

He sipped at his drink. 'At the time of transfer, those shares were worth around fifty thousand dollars. They're worth twice that today, so naturally I was curious about it. It was the first time I had noticed Brady giving anything away. I did some checking.

'Sandra's mother had been a maid in Brady's home in Pittsburgh. From all I was able to find out she was a great deal like her daughter.' She smiled. 'Or more properly, it's the other way around. She was built, if you know what I mean.'

I nodded. I knew what he meant.

'Matt Brady was about fifty years old then. He had married late and almost before he had settled into it his wife was injured in an auto accident and became a permanent invalid. A woman like Marta could put quite a strain on a man, even one whose wife wasn't sick. You can imagine what happened.'

His drink was about half gone. I made to refill it but he shook his head. 'She had been working for Brady about three years when she suddenly left. Brady's wife was surprised by the short notice but gave Marta a nice gift anyway.

'About three months later Joe Wolenciwicz came up to Matt Brady's office, still in his work clothes. What the two men spoke about in that office I don't know. They were old friends, having worked together in the foundries many years before. I do know that Joe left that office with Matt Brady's personal cheque for five thousand dollars.

'He went from the office to his rooming house, where he changed into his only good suit. Then he went downtown to City Hall and met Marta. They were married that afternoon.

'Forty days later, Sandra was born. The very next day, Matt Brady transferred the stock.'

I sat quietly, staring into my glass. One thing about

Brady, he wasn't a piker about things. He was willing to pay for his ducal privileges. But it was more than that, really. In his own peculiar way he loved Sandra. She was his only issue. Now I understood why he wouldn't let her out of his sight. Outside of business, it was perhaps the only reminder that he had been a man.

I poured out another shot and sipped it. The strange kicks that life would take. The same possessiveness that made Brady want to keep his daughter close made her hate him. I wondered if he knew how she felt – and if he did, if it would make any difference to him.

'Circumstantial evidence, as you lawyers would say,' I said. 'You get some mighty good cases that way,' he smiled.

My mind was made up. There was no other way. I had to try for the knockout punch. 'How long would it take you to get copies of all the pertinent data?' I asked.

'A few hours,' he answered. 'I have some of them. Those pertaining to the stock transfer. The other stuff I'd have to get in Pittsburgh.'

I walked across the room and put the bottle back in the liquor cabinet. 'Get it,' I said. 'I'll meet you in Matt Brady's office tomorrow afternoon at one o'clock.'

A strange look came into his face. He started to speak, but hesitated.

'What's the matter?' I asked. 'Afraid?'

He shook his head. 'Not for me. I've already had it. But you?'

I stood silently for a minute. I knew what he meant. But there was no other way. Finally I smiled. 'What's the rap in Pennsylvania for blackmail?'

His face was straight as he answered. 'I don't know off-hand.'

'Check that too while you're down there,' I said. 'Might as well know what'll happen if I lose.'

The desk clerk at the Towers smiled at me. 'Good evening, Mr Rowan.'

I looked at the clock on the wall behind him. It was after nine. 'Would you check Mrs Schuyler for me, please.'

'Certainly, Mr Rowan.' He picked up the phone and spoke into it. After a few seconds he looked up. 'She doesn't answer, sir.' He looked in the rack behind him. There was a key there. He turned back to me. 'She must have gone out before I came on.'

I nodded and held out my hand for the key. 'She'll probably be back any minute. I'll wait for her.'

'It's most irregular, sir.' He hesitated until he saw the bill in my hand, then his voice changed suddenly. 'But I suppose it will be all right, seeing as how it's you,' he wound up with a smile, exchanging the key for the fiver.

I thanked him and went up to her suite. I let myself in and turned the light on. I left my hat and coat on a chair near the door and made myself a Scotch and water. The room was warm and I opened the window slightly and sat down opposite it.

The noise of the city rose vaguely to my ears as I sipped the drink. I wondered if she knew about Sandra. Probably not, or she would have told me long before. Or would she? Matt Brady was still her flesh and blood.

It was almost ten when I got up for my second drink and she hadn't come in yet. I turned on the radio and sat down again. I was tired and my eyes were burning. I killed the light and sat there in the dark. The music was soft and soothing. I could feel my nerves begin to ease.

I set the drink carefully on the table next to me and dozed...

Somewhere in the distance I could hear *The Star-Spangled Banner*. I struggled to open my eyes. They were heavy with sleep. I hit the light and it flooded into the room. The music was coming from the radio. The station was signing off for the night. I looked at my watch. It was three o'clock.

I got to my feet and turned off the radio. I hadn't realised I was so tired. I wondered where she was. On a hunch I walked into the bedroom and opened her closet.

I had been right. Her travelling bag was gone. I shut the closet and went back into the other room. I picked up my hat and coat and let myself out. There was a peculiar hurt inside me as I went down in the elevator. At least she owed me the chance to explain. I tossed the key on the desk and went outside to pick up a cab.

Chapter TWENTY-SEVEN

Marge came into the room while I was dressing. I was standing in front of the mirror, knotting my tie. I was making my fourth pass at getting it to fall right and swore softly under my breath.

'Let me do it,' she said quickly.

I turned and she tied it swiftly and patted it into place. 'Only man in the world with ten thumbs.' She smiled.

I looked down at her wondering whether the war was

over. It was the first nice word she had for me all week. 'No reason for me to change now,' I smiled back. 'I'm too old.'

She looked up into my face, a certain wistfulness in her eyes. 'I'm not too sure about that,' she said slowly. 'You've changed in some ways.'

I knew what she meant but I didn't want to renew the argument. 'I'm going down to Pittsburgh this morning to see Brady,' I said.

'Something breaking?' she asked hopefully.

'Uh-uh,' I said carefully. 'Just the last chance. I gotta win today or fold.'

She looked away. 'It's that bad?'

'Yeah. The business is shot and the bills are beginning to pile up.'

'What are you going to say to him?'

I picked up my jacket from the bed and shrugged into it. 'I'm goin' to try a little blackmail, that's all.'

A concern came into his voice. 'Is it dangerous?'

'A little,' I answered. 'But I have nothing more to lose now.'

She didn't answer right away. Absently she smoothed the bed-cover. 'The business mean that much to you?'

'We gotta eat,' I answered. 'You can't bring up kids on hot air.'

'We could get along with less if we had to,' she said. 'It would be better than your getting into more trouble.'

I laughed. 'I won't get into any more trouble. I've had the whole package.'

'I hope you know what you're doing,' she said doubtfully.

'I'll be okay,' I reassured her.

We started for the door and went silently down the

steps. While we were sitting at the table waiting for the coffee, Jeanie came in. She went over to Marge and kissed her cheek.

'Bye, Mummy.'

She went back past me and started out to the door.

'Wait a minute, baby,' I said. 'I'll take you down to school as soon as I get some coffee.'

She looked at me coldly for a moment, and then she spoke, 'No, thank you, Dad,' she said formally. 'I'm meeting some kids on the bus.' She turned quickly and ran out.

I looked over at Marge. The sound of the front door closing came back to my ears. For a moment I almost felt like a stranger in my own house.

'She's still a child, Brad,' Marge said quickly. 'There're some things she doesn't understand.'

I didn't speak. Sally put the coffee down and I raised the cup to my lips. The hot liquid burned my throat and warmed me a little.

'Is Mrs Schuyler going to be there?' Marge asked.

I shook my head.

'What does she think about your idea?' she continued. 'Does she approve?'

'She doesn't know anything about it,' I answered. 'She left the city last night.'

Marge raised an inquiring eyebrow. 'Where'd she go?'

'How should I know?' I asked peevishly. 'I got enough troubles of my own without keeping track of her.'

A faint smile crossed her lips. 'I'm sorry, Brad,' she said. 'I didn't mean to pry.'

I had enough coffee. I got up. 'I'm going,' I said.

She sat there looking up at me. 'When will you be back?'

'Tonight,' I said. 'If there's any change I'll call you.' I started for the door.

'Brad!' She came towards me, her face turned up to mine. 'Good luck.'

I kissed her cheek. 'Thanks,' I said. 'I'll need it.'

Her arm caught around my neck. 'No matter what happens, Brad,' she whispered quickly. 'Just remember that we're all pulling for you.'

I stared down into her eyes, trying to see what went on inside her pretty little head.

She turned her face and rested it on my chest. I could hardly hear her. 'I mean it, Brad,' she whispered. 'I have no complaints, no matter what happens. None of us comes with a lifetime guarantee.'

'Marge,' I said huskily.

'Don't speak, Brad,' she whispered quickly. 'Just be right, no matter what you do. When you finally make up your mind, tell me. I'll try to help.' She took her arms from around my neck and ran into the kitchen.

I stood there, staring at the swinging door. Slowly it stopped and I went out to the car.

I drove right out to the airport and called the office from there. 'Did you hear from Levi yet?' I asked Mickey.

'Yes,' she answered. 'He said he'd meet you at Pittsburgh airport.'

'Did he get everything?' I asked.

'He didn't say,' she answered.

'Any other calls?'

'Nothing important,' she answered. 'Wait a minute. Oh yes, Mrs Schuyler called from Washington. She wants you to call her.'

I checked my watch. I would just have time to make the plane. 'I'll call her from Pittsburgh,' I said quickly. 'I gotta run.'

I put down the phone and went to the plane. I was feeling better. She had called me. I began to whistle as I walked across the field.

Chapter TWENTY-EIGHT

The cab dropped us just outside the steel gate. We walked through and into the building. The special officer eyed Bob's briefcase sceptically as we stopped in front of his desk.

'Mr Rowan to see Mr Brady,' I told him.

The big clock was just at one o'clock when he picked up the phone. He looked up at us. 'Mr Brady is tied up,' he said. 'He refers you to Mr Proctor.'

I didn't come to see Chris. 'May I speak to Mr Brady's secretary?' I asked.

He spoke into the phone again, then put down the receiver. He gave me a curious look and waved us over to the elevator. The doors opened and we got in.

Sandy was waiting in the corridor as we got out. 'Brad!' she said in a hushed voice. 'What are you doing down here?'

I waited until the elevator doors had closed behind us. Then I started down the corridor towards the office. 'I want to see your boss.'

'You can't go in,' she said. 'He's got Mr Proctor with him.'

'Good,' I grinned. 'I was told to see Mr Proctor.' I opened the door of her office and walked on through to Brady's door.

Her hand caught at my arm. 'Please don't, Brad,' she begged. 'He'll only make it worse for both of us.' There was terror in her eyes.

I looked at her. I could feel her hand trembling on my arm. I could feel anger rising in me. What kind of a man was he to make another human feel so frightened and insecure? And though she didn't know it, it was even worse in her case. She was his daughter. I put my hand over hers gently.

'Sandy,' I said softly. 'You don't have to be afraid of him any more. When we leave this office, he won't be any different from any of us.'

Her eyes were wide. 'What are you going to do?'

'Show him that he's not God,' I said, opening the door.

Chris was sitting with his back to the door, facing Brady behind his desk. Brady saw us first. He began to get to his feet angrily. 'I told you I didn't want to see you,' he said coldly.

'I wanted to see you,' I said, stepping into the office. I heard Bob come in after me and close the door.

'You were told to report to Mr Proctor,' Brady said.

Chris was on his feet now, staring at me. I let my gaze go right through him. 'I report to nobody,' I said. 'Least of all the office boy.'

I started towards the desk. Chris made a move as if to stop me. I looked at him coldly and he stepped back to let me pass. I could see Brady's hand moving towards the buzzer on his desk. 'I wouldn't call your policemen if I were you, Brady,' I said quickly. 'You might live to regret it.'

His hand froze over the buzzer. 'What do you mean?'

I lowered the boom. 'Do you know that your daughter hates you?'

His face was suddenly white. I could feel him staring deep into me, burning into my mind. We were the only two people in the room now.

His tongue ran over his lips, trying to moisten their dryness. His lips moved. 'You're lying!' he exploded, the colour flooding back into his face.

Chris's voice came over my shoulder. 'You may as well leave, Brad. Mr Brady isn't interested in your idle threats.'

I didn't even turn to look at him. I still watched Brady. 'I'm not lying, Brady,' I said. 'I can prove it.'

'He was just telling me to give you every consideration possible, but under the present circumstances, even crawling on your hands and knees wouldn't help,' Chris continued.

For the first time since I came into the office I looked at him. This was one place his arithmetic wasn't going to do him any good. 'I learned a lot of things from you,

Chris,' I said coldly. 'But not crawling. That's your speciality.'

Chris looked over at Brady. 'Shall I call the guards, sir?' he asked.

Brady was still staring at me. He spoke as if he hadn't heard. 'I tried to do everything I could for her, saw that she had everything she needed. A home. Money.'

Suddenly I saw him as a tired old man robbed of his only child. I thought of my Jeanie, and a strange sympathy for him came into me. 'People are not like a business, Brady,' I said softly. 'You can't buy and sell them like so much property. You can't lock them up in a vault and expect them to appreciate it.'

I could see his fingers white on his desk. There seemed to be no blood in his hands. 'I asked how you knew, Mr Rowan?'

'She came into my office last night and begged me to find her a place where she could be free of you,' I answered.

His words came very slowly. 'Does she know about the relationship?'

I shook my head. 'No.'

'You didn't tell her?'

I didn't mention that I hadn't found out until after she had gone. 'It wasn't my place, Mr Brady. You're her father; I'm only her friend.'

He stared down at his hands for a long time. At last he looked up. 'Proctor, go back to your office,' he said. 'I'll call you if I need you.'

Sheer hatred glared out of Chris's eyes towards me at his summary dismissal. I smiled at him pleasantly. It only seemed to make him more infuriated as he stalked out. I turned back to Brady.

'Sit down, Mr Rowan,' he said wearily.

I took the chair that Chris had vacated. Brady's gaze went past me to Bob. There was no recognition in the look. 'My associate, Mr Robert M. Levi,' I said.

Brady nodded, still with no recognition.

'You may remember him,' I added. 'He was the young attorney who prepared the anti-trust case against your company.'

A subtle change came into Matt Brady's face; it seemed almost contemptuous. 'I remember now,' he said, turning to me. 'We paid him twenty-five thousand dollars to leave the government.'

I looked up at Bob. 'That's not the way I heard it,' I said.

There was a flush on his face. 'I never took a cent, Brad,' he said angrily.

I turned back to Brady. 'I believe him, Brady.'

'I personally reimbursed the private detective I hired to check on him when he told me that was the only way we could get him to leave,' Brady snapped.

'Then you've been had, Brady,' I answered. 'Bob left the government at your insistence but not for that reason. It was to protect his wife from your threats. He was offered money but never took any part of it.'

He looked at Bob. Bob nodded. 'That was the only reason that could make me quit. I didn't want any part of your money.'

Brady closed his eyes wearily. 'I don't know what to believe.' He looked up at Bob. 'But if I'm wrong, I'm sorry.'

Brady turned back to me. 'How did you find out about Sand – er – my daughter, Mr Rowan? I thought it was pretty well hidden by now.'

I nodded at Bob. 'I was pretty desperate, Mr Brady,' I answered. 'I went to Bob and asked his help. It was he who actually found out. The stock transfer you made to her the day after she was born was what gave it away. He came across it while working on the case.'

'I see,' he nodded. 'You are like me, Mr Rowan. I believe I said that once before. You're a fighter.'

I didn't answer.

He folded his hands on his desk. 'I suppose I should have told Norah a long time ago,' he said almost to himself, 'but I couldn't. I was afraid it would kill her. She's an invalid and very proud. If she felt that she hadn't given me all that I wanted she would die.'

He spun his chair around and looked out the large window at the smoking foundries behind him. 'I couldn't tell Nora and I couldn't let my daughter leave me. I had to find a way to see her every day.' There was a faint bitterness in his voice. 'I'm an old man now. The doctor says I should have quit a long time ago. But I couldn't.' He spun his chair back and looked at me. 'The only reason I still come in to work is to see her. Even if it's only for a few minutes each day.

'Why once when she left me and took a job somewhere else, I found out she wasn't making enough to live on. I made her come back. I didn't want her to have to struggle.' His voice trailed away. For a few moments he was silent, then he looked up at me again. 'But it seems everything I did was wrong,' he added.

Bob and I looked at each other and remained silent. The minutes ticked slowly away while the old man sat at his desk and looked at his hands. I took out a cigarette and lit it.

'You've managed to get yourself pretty well involved with my family, Mr Rowan,' Brady said suddenly.

I knew what he meant. 'Mrs Schuyler is a very good

friend,' I said. 'I'm trying to help her on the Infantile drive.'

'You've been seeing quite a lot of her, according to the papers,' he said.

I smiled. 'You know the papers. They're always looking for something to print.'

'I thought you might be playing up to her because of me,' he said flatly.

'I happened to be very fond of Elaine, long before I knew either you or that she was related to you. She's a brave, wonderful person and she's had more than enough trouble. I'm very proud that she likes me.'

He looked into my eyes. 'I know she thinks a great deal of you.'

I didn't answer.

'That doesn't settle the matter you came to see me on,' he said.

'It doesn't,' I agreed.

'If I didn't agree to work with you,' he guessed shrewdly, 'you planned to bring out that business with my daughter into the open, didn't you?'

'It was something like that,' I admitted.

'And if I still refuse?' he asked.

I thought for a long moment, then I answered. 'Many years ago my father told me I could choose between a hell now or a hell hereafter. I didn't know what he meant then but I'm beginning to learn. I'd rather my hell came hereafter.'

'Then you're not going to say anything?' he asked, his eyes on my face.

I shook my head. 'That's not my affair. It's your own private hell. I want no part of it.'

A slight sigh escaped his lips. 'I'm glad you said that. If

you had threatened me, I would have had to fight you no matter what happened.'

I got to my feet. 'That's the way I felt about you the last time I was down here.' I started for the door. 'Come on, Bob,' I said.

'Wait a minute, Mr Rowan.'

I turned back towards the desk. 'Yes?'

The little man was on his feet, his usually reserved face was warm with a smile. 'How are we going to be able to work out the details of the account if you leave?'

I could feel my heart pumping with excitement. I made it – I made it. The long shot paid off. I didn't speak.

He came around the desk towards me. I took his outstretched hand. He opened the door. 'Sandra, please come in here.'

She came into the room, a questioning look in her face. 'Yes, Mr Brady?'

'Mr Rowan's firm is undertaking the public relations campaign for us. I thought it might be a good idea if you went to New York to keep an eye on it for me.' There was a strange pleading in his eyes as he looked at her.

She looked at him for a moment, then glanced at me out of the corner of her eye. Almost imperceptibly I shook my head. 'Later,' I made silently with my lips, from behind him.

She had enough of her father in her to catch on quickly. She smiled at the old man. 'If it's all right with you, Mr Brady,' she said quickly, 'I'd rather stay here with you for a while.'

The old man couldn't hide his pleasure. The radiant smile on his face was bright enough to light up the whole room.

Chapter TWENTY-NINE

It was one of those garden apartments that dot the fashionable sections just off the outskirts of Washington. The hall light was out, so I struck a match while I checked the bell.

Schuyler. I punched the button. Somewhere deep in the house I could hear a chime tinkling. The match flared out and I waited in the darkness. After a few minutes I hit the button again. But there was no answer. The house still remained dark.

I went back out of the hall and sat down on the steps. It was sheer madness, and I knew it. Even if she had called me from home as Mickey had told me, there was no reason for her to be there now. For all I knew she could have gone off someplace for the week-end. After all, it was Friday night.

I lit a cigarette. Maybe I was off on the wrong kick altogether. Could be I wasn't so sharp after all. Maybe she was conning me all the time. Maybe there was another guy – even other guys. I didn't know. All I knew was what she told me. And there was nothing in the book that said she couldn't lie to me if she wanted to.

The cigarette turned bitter in my mouth and I threw it away. Its sparks scattered on the cement walk in front of me like a hundred little fireflies. The night was turning chill and I pushed my coat collar up around my neck. There was nothing else I could do. I was ready to sit there until Doomsday if I had to.

It had been like that back at the airport in Pittsburgh when I tried to call her and there had been no answer. Even then I knew I would have to see her. There was no other way out for me. So I bought me a plane ticket to Washington and called home instead.

I tried to keep my voice light while I spoke to Marge. 'Baby,' I lied. 'Brady says I got the deal, but I gotta see the institute president in Washington tonight.'

'Can't it keep until Monday?' she asked. 'I've such a terrible feeling about this week-end.' I could almost see her knit her brows together the way she did when she felt low.

'It can't, honey,' I said quickly, compounding the felony. 'You know the job is the last hope we had. Until Brady said okay we were dead. I can't afford to let anything go wrong now.'

I had the strangest feeling she didn't believe me. I could hear her breath hit the phone. 'Okay, Brad,' she said hesitantly. 'If you have to –'

'Of course, I have to,' I jumped in. 'If I didn't I wouldn't go. You know that.'

Her voice was very small. 'I don't know anything any more, Brad,' she said and rang off.

I put the phone back on the hook and walked thoughtfully out on the field. The Washington plane was just coming in and it got me there a little after nine o'clock. It was almost ten when I first rang her bell . . .

From somewhere behind the apartment came the sound of an automobile motor, then a garage door closed. For a few seconds there was silence, then the sounds of high heels against a cement walk came from around the corner of the building.

I scrambled to my feet and faced the sound. My legs were trembling suddenly. She came around the corner, but she didn't see me.

The moon was full on her face and there was a beautiful, sad loneliness etched into it that my heart was strangely glad to see. 'Elaine!' I whispered.

She stopped, her hand clutched at her throat. 'Brad!' she breathed, and a sudden joy appeared on her face and as quickly disappeared.

She came towards me. Her voice was low and taut. 'Brad, why did you come? We both know it's over.'

'I had to see you,' I said. 'You couldn't walk out on me just like that.'

She stopped a few feet away from me, her eyes fixed on my face. 'Haven't you done enough?' she cried. 'Made me cheap and common like all the others? Can't you leave well enough alone?'

'That girl means nothing to me,' I said. 'She was just

being grateful because I promised to help her.'

She didn't speak, just stared at me with dark, pain-filled eyes. There was something in their depths that told me she wanted to believe me.

I reached a hand towards her but she stepped back. 'Tell me that you don't love me,' I said. 'And I'll go.'

'Go away,' she whispered in a tight, bitter voice. 'Leave me alone!'

'I can't,' I said. 'You mean everything to me. I can't let you go like this. Only if you tell me you don't love me.'

She looked down at the ground. 'I don't love you,' she said in a small voice.

'It seems like only a few days ago you said you loved me,' I said. 'You looked up into my eyes and said you loved me with all your heart. You said that nobody ever made you feel so loved and loving.

'Look at me now and tell me that you lied. Tell me that you don't love me today; tell me that you can turn on and off like you can water in a faucet. Then I'll believe you.'

Slowly her face turned up to mine. I could see her lips trembling. 'I – I – ' She couldn't speak.

I held my arms towards her and she came into them quickly. Her face was against my coat and she was crying, hard bitter sobs that shook her whole body. I could hardly make out what she was saying. 'For a moment ... back there in the office ... that girl was me ... and I was your wife ... suddenly I was so ashamed. It was so wrong ... so very wrong.'

I held her very tight and close to me. Her hair brushed my lips as I whispered to her. I could feel my tears running down my cheeks into her hair. 'Please, Elaine,' I begged. 'Please don't cry.'

Her lips were pressing wildly against mine. 'Brad, Brad,

I love you so!' she cried, her kisses salty in my mouth. 'Don't let me run away from you again! Never leave me!'

'That's it, darling,' I said, suddenly content. I closed my eyes against her kiss. 'I'll never leave you.'

Chapter THIRTY

It was a week-end to throw away the clock. Time meant nothing. It was the honeymoon that never happened, the dream that never was true. We were together like no two people ever were; we ate when we thought of it, slept when we were exhausted.

We drew a curtain about our lives and the only real things in it were the way we felt about each other. We laughed at all the silly normal things of life: shaving, bathing, dressing, coffee bubbling over the pot, toast burning. It was a private world, created by ourselves for our own delight.

But like all things that man had made, it came to an end. Maybe a little sooner than we had planned, but the time was coming close anyway and we both knew it, even if we didn't talk about it. And then, when we had started to talk about it, the telephone rang and the week-end burst like a bubble in our faces.

I was stretched on the floor in front of the open fireplace. The heat of the flames was licking out at me and I stretched lazily. She had just come out of the shower and was walking around me. I never saw such a dame for showers. She was shower-happy. Could take one every minute.

The flame cast a reddish gold glow on her legs where they stuck out beneath the towel. I rolled over and made a grab for her and she tumbled down beside me, laughing. I laughed with her, pulling the towel away. She fought to hold it close but not too hard.

Her eyes were sombre as they looked at me. I kissed her tiny nose. She smiled a moment and then her eyes were sombre again. Her voice held its first trace of pain in two days. 'Brad, what's going to happen to us?'

It was a reasonable question, but it stopped me cold. She had a right to an answer. It was only that I had never really faced up to it. 'I don't know,' I said.

'We can't spend the rest of our lives like this,' she pointed out.

I tried for a funny. 'What's wrong with it? Seems great to me.'

She ignored it. 'You can't spend the rest of your life lying and hiding from people. Sooner or later you have to go out of the house.' She gathered up the towel. 'I don't know how you feel, but I'm not made for it.'

I lit a cigarette and blew the smoke out, then placed it between her lips. My answer came from the heart. 'I hate it, too.'

Then her eyes watching me, she asked quietly: 'What are we going to do, Brad?'

I thought for a long time before I answered. This was no week-end jaunt that you paid off with a gag; this was for real. I pushed my fingers through her hair. 'There's only one thing we can do,' I said, turning her face towards me. 'Get married.'

Her voice was very low and trembled slightly. 'You sure that's what you want, Brad?'

I took a deep breath. 'I'm sure.'

'More than anything in this world, I want to live with you, be with you,' she said, her eyes still holding mine. 'But what about your wife? The children?'

A pain was growing inside me. I had thought about many things, but not about them. Now I realised I had been concerned only about myself. I looked down into her face. 'I didn't come looking for you, nor you for me,' I said. I remembered what Marge had told me that morning I left to see Brady. I knew now that Marge had the answer before I did. 'I think Marge already knows how I feel about you. The other day she said that nobody comes with lifetime guarantees. She would be the first not to want us to be any other way.'

She leaned her head against my breast. 'Say that's the way she feels, you still haven't said anything about the children.'

'They're not children any more,' I answered. 'They're grown people. Jeanie's sixteen and Brad's almost nineteen. They know all the facts of life. I'm sure they'll understand. They're almost at an age where they can take care of themselves.'

'But supposing they resent what you do and want nothing to do with you? How will you feel? Maybe after a while you'll begin to hate me for having taken you away from them.' Her voice was almost muffled against my chest.

There was a tightness in my throat. I could hardly speak. 'I – I don't think that would happen.'

'But it might,' she insisted. 'It has happened before.'

I didn't want to think about it. 'I'll face that when I have to.'

'And there's the money,' she persisted.

'What about it?' I asked quickly, a suspicion in my mind that her answers washed away.

'A divorce will cost you a lot of money,' she replied. 'I know you. You'll bend over backwards to be fair to her. Give her everything she wants, and it's only right that you should. She's entitled to that for all the years you've been together. But later, you might resent having given her all that money because of me.'

'I didn't have much when I started,' I said. 'It's okay with me if I don't have much when I go.' I smiled at her. 'That is – if you don't mind.'

She squeezed my hand. 'I don't care about money. Only you. I want you to be happy, no matter what.'

I kissed her hand. 'You'll make me happy.'

She pulled my face towards her and kissed my lips. 'I will, I will,' she promised.

I leaned back against a chair. 'I'll talk to Marge to-morrow.'

'Maybe – ' she hesitated a little. 'Maybe you ought to wait a while, to be sure.'

'I'm sure now,' I answered confidently. 'Delaying won't help. It will only make things worse.'

'What will you say to her?' she asked.

220

I started to answer but she suddenly put a finger to my lips, keeping me silent. 'No,' she said quickly. 'Don't tell me. I don't want to hear it. You're going to say what every woman faces in her secret heart, in her most terrible nightmares. We live in dread that one day he will come and say that he no longer cares.

'I don't want to hear what you'll say to her. Only promise me one thing, darling.' Her eyes looked deep into mine.

'What's that?' I asked.

'Be gentle with her, be kind to her,' she whispered. 'And never say it to me.'

'I promise,' I answered, kissing her brow.

'You'll never get tired of me, Brad?'

'Never,' I replied as the telephone began to ring.

We parted, startled. It was the first time it had rung all week-end. She looked at me questioningly. 'I wonder who it could be?' she asked. 'No one knows I'm home this week-end.'

I smiled at her. 'There's only one way to find out.'

She got up and picked up the phone. 'Hello,' she said. There was a crackling in the phone against her ear and a strange look came on to her face. Her voice grew cold and distant. 'Why no, I haven't seen him.' She looked at me peculiarly.

The phone crackled again. Her eyes widened as she listened and a terrible hurt came into them. The kind of hurt I had seen deep in their shadows the first day I saw her. She closed her eyes for a moment and swayed slightly.

I jumped to my feet and put an arm around her, steadying her. 'What's wrong?' I whispered.

A strained look appeared on her face. 'Never mind, Mr Rowan,' she said in a suddenly numb voice. 'He's here. I'll put him on.' She held the phone towards me.

I took it from her. 'Dad?' I said into the mouthpiece, my eyes following her as she crossed the room away from me.

He was trying to be calm. 'Marge told me to try to find you. Junior is very sick. She's flying out to him now.'

I could feel the room rocking under my feet. 'What's wrong?'

'Polio,' he answered. 'He's in the hospital. Marge said that you should pray for all of us.'

I couldn't speak for a moment.

His voice came nervously through the phone. 'Brad! Brad, are you all right?'

'I'm here,' I answered. 'When did Marge leave?'

'This afternoon. She told me to try to get you.'

'Where's Jeanie?' I asked.

I heard the click on the phone. 'I'm here, Dad,' her voice answered.

'Get off that phone, you little tyke!' I heard my father yell.

'It's okay, Dad,' I said. She must have been listening in on the upstairs extension. She would have to know sooner or later. 'How are you feeling, honey?'

She began to cry into the phone.

'Easy, baby,' I said gently. 'That won't help. I'll get right out there and see what I can do.'

'You will, Daddy?' There was an incredulous note of faith in her voice. 'You're not leaving us?'

I closed my eyes. 'Of course not, baby,' I said. 'Now get off the phone and go to bed. I want to talk to Gramps.'

Her voice was brighter now. 'Night, Daddy.'

'Good night, sweetie.' I heard the click of the phone. 'Pop,' I said.

'Yes, Bernard.'

'I'm leaving now. Anything you want me to tell Marge?'

'No,' he said. 'Only that I'm prayin' with you.'

I put down the phone, a bitter taste in my mouth. Marge hadn't called, because she knew. Pop called because he knew. The only one I had been fooling was myself.

I crossed the room to Elaine. 'You heard?' I asked.

She nodded. 'I'll drive you out to the airport.'

'Thanks,' I said. I walked towards the bathroom. 'I'll have to dress,' I said stupidly.

She didn't answer. She turned and walked into the bedroom. A few minutes later she came into the bathroom already dressed. I looked at her in the mirror while I knotted my tie. It didn't come out right but this was one time I didn't care.

There was a sympathy on her face. 'I'm terribly sorry, Brad,' she said.

'They say if they catch it early enough, it's not serious,' I said.

She nodded. 'They're much better with it now than they were when we – ' The memory brought the pain back to her eyes.

'Darling.' I turned and caught her to me.

She pushed me back. 'Hurry, Brad.'

At the plane, I kissed her. 'I'll call you, dear.'

She looked up into my face. 'I'm a Jonah,' she said sombrely. 'I'm bad luck for everyone I love.'

'Don't be silly,' I said. 'It's not your fault.'

Her eyes were wide on mine. 'I wonder,' she said.

'Elaine!' I said sharply.

Some of the introspection left her eyes. 'I'll pray that he's well.' She turned and ran back to her car.

I went into the plane and found a window seat. I peered through the window, but I couldn't see her. The

223

engine began to roar. I leaned forward and put my head in my hands. There was a crazy thought running through my mind. If it was anyone's fault, it wasn't Elaine's. It was mine.

What was it they said about the sins of the fathers?

Chapter THIRTY-ONE

It was almost midnight, Central Standard Time, when I gave my name to the blue-uniformed nurse at the reception desk in the hospital. I slipped out of my topcoat while she checked the card file in front of her. Through the door I could see the taxi that had brought me from the airport pull away from the hospital.

A nun in a grey habit walked by the desk. 'Sister Angelica,' the receptionist called.

The nun turned back. 'Yes, Elizabeth?'

'This is Mr Rowan,' the nurse introduced us. 'Would you mind taking him up to eight-twenty-two? His son is there.'

The nun's face was gentle. 'Follow me, please,' she said softly.

We went up in a self-service elevator. 'There are no operators on after ten o'clock,' she apologised, pressing the button.

We left the elevator in the eighth floor and started down a blue-painted hallway. There was another corridor off the main hall. We turned into it. Down at its end, I could make out a small figure huddled on a bench outside one of the rooms.

I broke into a run, leaving the nun behind me. 'Marge!' I cried.

She lifted her face as I came up to her. Lines of worry and exhaustion were etched deep into it. 'Brad!' she spoke huskily. It was a voice that had known many tears that day. 'Brad, you're here!'

She swayed and would have fallen if I hadn't caught her. 'How is he?' I asked anxiously.

She began to cry. 'I don't know. The doctors say it's too soon to tell. He hasn't reached the crisis yet.' She looked up at me, her grey eyes reminding me of Elaine. They were filled with the same kind of pain.

I couldn't face those eyes. I looked at the closed door, 'Can we see him?' I asked.

'They said we can peek in at midnight,' she answered.

'It's almost that now.' I turned to the nun questioningly.

'I'll get the doctor,' she said. She went back down the hall and vanished into one of the rooms.

'You'd better sit down.' I steered Marge back to the bench and sat down with her.

Her face was pale and drawn. I lit a cigarette and

placed it between her lips. She dragged on it nervously.

'Have you eaten anything yet?' I asked.

She shook her head. 'I couldn't. I have no appetite.'

Footsteps were coming down the hall. We looked up. Sister Angelica was returning with a doctor. 'You can look in now,' he said gently. 'But only for a minute.' He held the door open for us.

Silently we stepped through the doorway. I heard Marge draw in her breath as we saw him, and I felt her nails grip into my hand.

His body was hidden in a massive iron lung; only the top of his head showed. His thick black hair was glistening and oily with perspiration. His eyes were closed tight in his paper-white face. A small black tube led from his nostril to an oxygen tank near by and his breathing was tortured and laboured.

Marge stepped forward to touch him, but the doctor stopped her with a whisper. 'Don't disturb him. He's resting, and he'll need all he can get.'

She stood quietly there, her hand in mine, while we looked at our son. Her lips were moving as if she were speaking to him, but no sound came from them.

I looked at Brad closely. This was my flesh and I could feel its pain. This was the giant sprung from my loins, and now he lay there helpless, a part of me whose suffering I could not lighten.

I remembered the last time I saw him before he left for school in the fall. I had jibed him about being too light to go out for the football team. With his height, I had said, he'd better concentrate on basketball. It was less dangerous and if he was any good, he could grab fifty grand a year from the gamblers.

I couldn't remember what he had answered, but I could

227

recall the shocked expression on his face that I would even joke about such a thing.

And now he was wrapped in a piece of metal that had to breathe for him because his body was too wracked to carry on. My baby. I used to walk the floor with him at night when he cried. The strongest lungs in the world, I used to complain. I wouldn't complain now. Nothing was strong enough. Not even I could breathe for him. Only a metal monster, whose white aseptic sides leered ominously in the hospital light.

'Better go now,' the doctor whispered.

I turned to Marge. She blew a kiss to the sleeping boy and I took her arm and followed the doctor out of the room. The door closed silently behind us.

'When will we know anything, Doctor?' I asked.

He shrugged his shoulders helplessly. 'Can't tell, Mr Rowan. He hasn't reached the crisis yet. Could be an hour or a week. It's anybody's guess.'

'Will he – will he be affected permanently?'

'We can't tell anything until after the crisis, Mr Rowan,' he answered. 'Once that's passed, we can check and find out whether any damage has been done. There's only one thing I can say to you now.'

'What's that, Doctor?' I asked eagerly.

'We're doing everything that is humanly possible. Try not to worry or anticipate anything. It won't help if you make yourself sick too.' He turned to Marge. 'You've been here for a long time,' he said gently. 'Time you got some rest.'

She brushed the back of her hand across her eyes. 'I'm not tired.'

'Make her rest, Mr Rowan,' he said to me. 'You can see your son again at eight in the morning. Good night.' He turned and went down the hall.

We watched him go back into his room, then I turned to Marge. 'You heard the doctor,' I said.

She nodded.

'Come on, then,' I said. 'What hotel are we at?'

'I didn't bother,' she said dully. 'I came right from the airport.'

'There's a telephone downstairs that you can use,' Sister Angelica said. 'You can call a hotel from there.'

I thanked her. 'Where is your bag?' I asked Marge.

'At the reception desk,' she answered.

Slowly we walked back to the elevator. We came out of the elevator and went to the reception desk. 'The phone is straight down the corridor,' Sister Angelica told me.

I left them at the desk while I went to the telephone and called a hotel and a cab. When I came back, they weren't there. I leaned over the desk. 'My wife?' I asked the nurse.

She looked up at me from a magazine on the shelf in front of her. 'I believe she went to the chapel with Sister Angelica, Mr Rowan,' she said, gesturing with her hand. 'It's just past the elevator, first door on your right.'

It was a small chapel, filled with a golden light from the many candles flickering on the altar. I stood in the doorway for a moment, looking in. Marge and Sister Angelica were at the rail, their heads bent forward. Slowly I walked down the little aisle and knelt beside Marge.

I looked at her. Her hands were clasped on the rail before her and her forehead touched her fingers. Her lips were moving and her eyes were closed, but she knew I was beside her. She moved slightly closer to me.

Chapter THIRTY-TWO

I lay quietly on my pillow, listening to Marge crying in her sleep. There was no sleep for me. I kept remembering what Marge had said before she finally succumbed to the exhaustion that had seeped all her strength.

'I'm so frightened, Brad,' she had wept.

'He'll be all right,' I said more confidently than I had felt. I could feel a strange band of tightness in my throat.

'Please, God,' she cried. 'I couldn't bear to lose him, too.'

Then I was sure that she knew and still I didn't speak. Words of reassurance rose to my lips, but I could say nothing about myself. Another time, another place, maybe. But not now.

I thought about Elaine. Now I could understand what she had meant. The years of living would take their toll. Now I knew why she had asked how I would feel.

Marge was still weeping softly in her sleep. A tenderness for her came over me that I had never felt before. I slipped my arm beneath her shoulders and drew her head to my breast.

She rested there, softly, lightly, like a child, and soon her weeping stopped. Her breath came easy and restfully. I lay there, waiting out the night until the day crept in the windows.

It was a week before we got the answer. Then, one morning, when we came into the hospital, everyone was smiling. Sister Angelica, the receptionist, the elevator operator, the orderlies and attendants who were usually grim and sober in their duties. All were smiling for us.

The doctor came out of his little office down the hall, his hands outstretched. I took one, Marge took the other. 'It's over,' he said happily. 'He'll be okay. A little rest and he'll be as good as new.'

We couldn't speak, only stare at each other with tear-filled eyes. Our free hands clung together tightly as we followed him down the hall to Brad's room.

He was lying on a bed, his head slightly raised on a pillow, facing the door. On the other side of the room was the big iron lung. Together we knelt at the side of his bed and kissed him and cried.

At last he smiled at us, a slightly weak version of his old grin. His hand moved on the sheet, pointing to the iron lung. 'Man!' he said faintly, but with all his usual spirit. 'Dig that crazy wind tunnel!'

I went right to the office from the airport. Dad was taking Marge and Junior directly home. It was a little before nine o'clock and the office was empty. I grinned to myself. There was a lot I had to catch up on. I closed the door to my office and began to go through the papers on my desk.

Bob Levi was going to be all right. He had stepped right in when I was gone. When the word went out that I was okay all my old customers wanted back in. He had taken them back, but at increased rates. I guess he felt they should pay for their crimes.

It was almost ten o'clock when I looked up. Where the devil was everybody. I punched down the switch on the intercom.

'Brad, is that you?' Mickey's voice was startled.

'It ain't a ghost!' I roared in my best Simon Legree manner.

Then everyone from the office boy up piled into my office and shook my hand. They were all happy for me. I felt good. Everything was going fine.

When they had left, Bob lingered behind. 'We have a twelve-thirty luncheon meeting with the Steel Institute committee,' he said.

'Okay,' I answered.

'And their attorney's promised to have the contract on your desk after lunch,' he added.

I looked up at him. 'I don't know what I would have done without you,' I said.

He smiled down at me. 'I feel the same way about you,' he said. 'Funny, isn't it?'

'But good,' I laughed.

He went back into his office and the morning worked on. Shortly before lunch, Mickey came into my office carrying a package.

'The furrier sent this over to you.' She placed it on my desk.

I looked at it. For a moment I didn't remember. Then it came back. Tomorrow was our anniversary. It was hard to believe that almost a month had gone since that morning I drove Jeanie down to school and she had put a bee in my bonnet. So much had happened.

'Have it put in the car,' I said to her.

She turned and took it out of the office with her. I watched the door close behind her. I had ordered it the morning I first met Elaine.

Elaine! My fingers froze on the desk. I had promised to call but never got the chance. A thousand years had passed since I spoke to her last. I picked up the phone and dialled long distance.

I was just about to give the operator her number when Bob stuck his head in the door.

'Better hurry,' he said. 'You don't want to be late for your first official meeting with them.'

Reluctantly I put down the phone and got up. I would call her right after lunch. I picked up my hat and coat and walked to the door.

I didn't know it then, but she had already been dead more than twelve hours.

THE BEGINNING AS THE END

My head ached and my eyes were burning with unshed tears. I don't know how long I sat there staring out the windows but I found no answer.

The buzzer hawked. Wearily I walked over to my desk and picked up the phone. 'Yes, Mickey.'

'Sandra Wallace is here to see you.'

I hesitated a moment. The clock on my desk said almost six. Then I made up my mind. 'Send her in,' I said.

I stood there as the door opened and Sandra came in. She was strong and blonde and vital. The basic forces of life were powerful in her. There was nothing in this world that could destroy her. I was sure of that. She was so different from Elaine.

Her blue eyes looked at me. 'Hello, Brad,' she said softly, standing just inside the door.

'Sandy,' I said gently. 'Come on in.'

She came slowly into the room. 'How are you?'

'Okay,' I said wearily.

'I'm glad your kid's better,' she said.

'Thanks,' I said. I wondered vaguely where she had learned about it. 'What brings you to town?'

'I have a message for you,' she said.

'From Mr Brady?' I asked.

She shook her head. 'No.'

I looked at her questioningly.

'From Mrs Schuyler,' she said.

For a moment the words didn't penetrate, then they burst in my brain. 'From Mrs Schuyler?' I said stupidly. 'But she's – she's –'

'I know,' Sandy said quietly. 'I heard about it this morning. Mr Brady was very upset.'

'How did you get a message from her?' I asked. 'Did you see her?'

She shook her head again. 'No. It came this morning in the mail.' She opened her pocketbook and took out an envelope. She held it towards me.

I took it from her and looked at it. The envelope was open. I looked up at her.

'The first one is mine,' she said quickly. 'There's another one inside. That's yours.'

I lifted the flap. The faint familiar scent of Elaine's perfume came to my nostrils. I closed my eyes. I could see her standing there before me. I pulled out the inside envelope. It was sealed. I slit the flap. I looked at Sandy. She was still standing.

'I'll wait outside,' she said quickly.

I shook my head. 'Stay here,' I said.

She went over to the couch and sat down. I sank into my chair and began to read Elaine's letter. Her hand was neat and orderly, it betrayed no excitement. Apparently her mind had already been made up when she sat down to write it. It was dated two days ago.

MY DEAREST BRAD,

Ever since I left you at the plane I have been thinking and praying for you constantly. My one great hope is that your son is well. That is the most important thing in the world.

It was in thinking of him I realised how small and foolish we had been, how selfish both of us really were. We, who were ready to sacrifice all our worlds for the sake of a moment's passion.

For in truth, that was all we could ever have for each other. I realised that too. My life had already gone and I was trying to borrow some of yours.

I think I may have mentioned that you reminded me of David, that you had the same qualities and the same regard and love for your family that he had for us.

That was what first drew me to you, but I didn't know it then. You were the same kind of people.

In my loneliness while you were gone I found my way to the cemetery where David and the children rest. I sat there on the bench and looked at the monument that already bears my name. It is a place at his side, the place at his side I always held in his life. It was then it came to me that if I were to be with you, I could never be with him and the children. We could never be together again; we who meant so much to each other!

That is how I found that I did not love you less, but that I loved David and my children more.

So please do not think that I have betrayed your love. I cherished it more than I could ever tell. Please think kindly of me and pray for me.

Love,
ELAINE.'

My eyes still burned from all the tears that day but I felt better now. There was a weight off my soul. I got to my feet. 'You're very kind to bring this to me, Sandy,' I said huskily.

She rose to her feet. 'I had to bring it,' she said. 'I knew that you loved her.'

I took a deep breath. 'I loved her,' I said. I just never knew how much pain she lived with, how hurt she had been. All I could remember now were her eyes, so smoky blue, almost violet with the pain swirling in their depths.

She was at the door. 'I've got to get back,' she said. 'I promised Aunt Nora I would be home by twelve.'

'Aunt Nora?' I asked, surprise creeping into my voice.

She nodded. 'Mr Brady took me home to meet her. He said he wants me to feel that I'm her daughter. I'm staying with them for a little while.' A curious smile crossed her lips. 'I wonder what you said to him that day. He's been a completely different person since. I'm even beginning to like him. He's actually a very gentle man when you get to know him.'

'I'm glad, Sandy,' I said, walking over to the door and

looking down at her. 'You'll be good for both of them now.'

'I hope so.' She smiled, holding her cheek up to me to be kissed like a little girl.

I kissed her. 'Bye, Sandy.'

The door closed behind her and I went over to the window and opened it. I stood there quietly and tore Elaine's letter into tiny little shreds, and let them flutter out of the window.

It was an end, but it also was a beginning. A new life and understanding for me. I was no different from many other guys who forgot that fall was the season of maturity and reached back desperately for the fires of spring. I knew better now. You can't turn back the clock. There was a lot of living to be done with Marge and the kids. Good living. Now I knew what Elaine had meant. A place at their side. I took a deep breath. The cold air went far into my lungs and felt good there. Suddenly I was anxious to be home ...

The first snow of the season began to fall as I drove home. It had just dusted the ground lightly by the time I turned into the driveway. I pulled in front of the garage and sat in the car, looking up at my house.

The lights were on in every window, even Brad's room, and a warm glow came from them. Dad's hack was parked in front of the door.

I got out of the car and opened the garage door. The hinges squeaked noisily, as usual. I got back into the car and drove it into the garage.

I heard Jeanie's voice calling me. 'Dad! Dad!'

I got out of the car and she ran into my arms. I kissed her lightly. 'How's my girl?' I asked.

'Great!' she answered excitedly, then lowered her voice to a conspiratorial whisper. 'I hope you didn't forget

Mother's present, because she's got the most beautiful wristwatch for you!' Her hand flew to her mouth. 'Oh gosh! I went and told you. And I promised I wouldn't!'

I smiled at her. She had probably told Marge about my gift. She couldn't keep a secret, never could. 'That's all right, honey,' I said gently. 'I won't let on.'

I reached across the seat and picked up the box with the furrier's seal and stuck it under my arm. Then, hand in hand, our heels scuffing the snow on the cement walk beneath our feet, we went up to the house.